A grave
IN THE AIR

A grave
IN THE AIR

STEPHEN HENIGHAN

thistledown press

Library and Archives Canada Cataloguing in Publication

Henighan, Stephen, 1960-
A grave in the air / Stephen Henighan.

Short stories.
ISBN 978-1-897235-29-4

I. Title.

PS8565.E5818G73 2007   C813'.54   C2007-904532-4

Cover photograph© Reuters/Corbis
Cover and book design by Jackie Forrie
Printed and bound in Canada

Thistledown Press Ltd.
633 Main Street
Saskatoon, Saskatchewan, S7H 0J8
www.thistledownpress.com

 Canada Council   Conseil des Arts
for the Arts   du Canada

 Canadian   Patrimoine
Heritage   canadien

Thistledown Press gratefully acknowledges the financial assistance of the Canada Council for the Arts, the Saskatchewan Arts Board, and the Government of Canada through the Book Publishing Industry Development Program for its publishing program.

A grave

IN THE AIR

CONTENTS

THE KILLING PAST

LIKE MOST OLD women, Aunt Philippa had been young. She had the photographs to prove it: dogeared black-and-white shots of a slender figure in tight ankle-length skirts, dark jackets snug over ruffled white blouses and the narrow-brimmed cloche hats that had been fashionable among young women in England in the late 1920s. Felt-domed, their downturned brims resembling earflaps, the hats looked like shadows of the helmets German infantrymen would wear ten years later. The similarity didn't occur to me while Aunt Philippa was showing me the photographs. I had no reason, then, to connect her youth with the outbreak of war. Her hand shaking, she passed me a photograph of herself standing next to a long black open car, one low-heeled sensible shoe poised on the flared mudguard. "The girl sitting in the back is your grandmother. She was quite a pretty little thing at that stage."

I had to trust Aunt Philippa's memory. To me the photographs looked opaque. The women's smooth faces barely peeped out from beneath the brims of their hats, the men were robust-looking and blank-faced, their suits as regular as uniforms. It would require a radar more subtle than I possessed to pinpoint the differences distinguishing the souls of these dashing, mummified figures — or even to ascertain that souls had existed behind the middle-class proprieties, dutiful church-going, private schools and sporting prowess; behind the hearty banter that revealed feelings only in reverse, through nearly untraceable twists of irony. Having been dispatched to England on various occasions as a child and an adolescent, I knew that banter. It rang inside me, surfaced in my turns of phrase, causing me to wonder occasionally where my words came from.

"I barely recognize Granny," I said, "but it's a great car."

"That was my twenty-first birthday present. Simmonds taught me to drive it. In those days, when you were given your first car, it was the family chauffeur's job to teach you to drive it."

Each time I visited Aunt Philippa, her encasement in the world of the photographs felt more complete. Her refusal to return to England had kept that world intact. She had been sent out to Canada in 1954 with her husband, who was looking after the Canadian interests of Dunlop. When Uncle Nigel died of a heart attack, Aunt Philippa had refused to be repatriated. It was her way of keeping Uncle Nigel alive: the England of her imagination would always contain a living Nigel. Perched high in a downtown Ottawa brownstone hemmed in by office towers, her apartment affording the barest glimpse of a corner of the Confederation Building on the western fringes of Parliament Hill, she seemed not to have noticed that the Red Ensign in front of the Parliament Buildings had been replaced by the maple leaf.

That London today was a city where people ate curry, prayed to Allah and listened to reggae, she had no notion. She had few friends, so far as I could judge, and though she and my parents were the only members of our immediate family in Canada, they had never been particularly close. Even before mobility became a problem for her, Aunt Philippa preferred to spend Christmas alone.

Then she surprised me by standing up. The curled fringe of her cardigan nestling against her belt, she took a step that carried her askew, more catty-corner than towards me. The hip replacement that had never really worked hardened the side of her skirt with a slanting thrust. Her height surprised me, conceding me a glimpse of the figure that young woman in the photographs must have cut when the length of her legs was still slinky elegance. Her white hair little more than a pale gloaming over the liver-spotted eggshell of her skull, Aunt Philippa scanned the shelves above her wedding picture. The dried-out spines of her generation's paperback popular novels — Nevil Shute, H.E. Bates, Jean Plaidy, Victoria Holt, Margery Allingham, Agatha Christie — ran up against a small wooden box. As I was thinking that I had seen those same paperback spines, in the same Pan, Fontana or Penguin editions, in countless houses in England, she said: "I could fetch it myself if I had to, but since you're here why don't you make yourself useful?"

Reaching up to remove the box from the shelf, I was relieved to see her sit down. "Don't you want to try the oatcakes and shortbread?" I asked.

"Not whilst you're here. I must ration my pleasures. Once you've gone I promise I shall eat until I make myself most ill."

"Don't do that, Aunt Philippa." I was unnerved. On my way over I had stopped off at the Marks and Spencer on Sparks Street — to buy a present for Aunt Philippa, I had told myself. Marks and Spencer, my mother once said, made emigration bearable. It made Canada less foreign, made us feel that we were still inhabiting an extension of Britain. At school in Ottawa I learned to recognize other boys with English parents by the telltale navy blue V-necked sweaters they wore over their shirts. Real Canadian boys responded to draughty corridors and chilly classrooms by putting on white T-shirts underneath their shirts, not sweaters over the top. I had also worn long, grey English school socks. At twenty-eight, I still wore them. I had spent more money at the shop on Sparks Street on three new pairs of grey socks for myself than I had on treats for Aunt Philippa.

"You're easily teased, aren't you, Bartholomew?" she said. "In my day we had great fun with chaps who were easily teased. Most of the girls could run rings around chaps like that."

"Did you run rings around chaps like that?" I asked.

"Oh, ever so easily," she said, straightening her shoulders. I thought about the young people in the last photograph: Aunt Philippa, my grandmother, who had been her younger sister, and two spiffily dressed, unidentified young men. I tried to imagine what the young women and the young men would have said to each other when they went out for a spin. Barred from doing many of the things that young men and women did together today, they had got their thrills from saucy conversation. When Aunt Philippa was alert, the memory of that way of using language persisted. "Doesn't your girl run rings around you? What's her name — Sharon?"

"That was the last one, Aunt Philippa. That's over."

"Oh, it's over, is it? And why is that?"

"I don't think we had much in common. I'm afraid it was mainly passion."

"And you have another one now?"

"Yes, Aunt Philippa. Karolina — you met her."

"Did I? She obviously didn't make an impression. Is Karolina just passion, too?"

"It's too early to tell — "

"You are horrible."

"Things are different now, Aunt Philippa."

"In my day a man who carried on was a cad. A man asked a girl to marry him quite early on. He made a commitment. And you knew that the baby would be born exactly nine months after the wedding."

"But, Aunt Philippa, that was decades ago." I held the box in my lap, feeling in need of biscuits to munch, a television screen to watch — a distraction to deflect this conversation. Aunt Philippa, as my mother liked to say, was a handful.

"It was no different for your parents. You were born nine months to the day after their wedding. That's why you were born in England, Bartholomew. Your mother had already come out to Canada not long after I had — I was supposed to be keeping an eye on her. But when she met your father and they went home to get married, it was nearly two years before your father could persuade your mother to come back to Canada."

"Yes, Aunt Philippa."

"Of course you know that, don't you? The trying part about being a living relic is that so few people remember what one remembers oneself. And when one tries to tell them they say, 'Listen to her going on like that, she must be senile.'"

The gaze behind the thick glasses took a wall-eyed amble in the direction of a stray pot of marmite abandoned on the counter of the kitchenette, her avoidance of my face strengthening the accusation. "Aunt Philippa, nobody — "

"Hand me that box. I'll tell you something you haven't heard before."

I passed her the box and watched her fingers fumbling at its engraved sides. When the lid popped up, she appraised the contents with a scowl. "I don't suppose," she said, "that you know how your great-grandfather tried to stop the Second World War?"

⁓

"Who was this guy?"

"His name was A.B. Chenvret. He was my great-grandfather."

"So he was, like, your Aunt Philippa's dad?"

"My Aunt Philippa's and my grandmother's. He died after the Second World War."

"Which he tried to stop. Bart, I know your family think they're important, but isn't this kind of pushing it?" Karolina looked up at the curl of light, fanning out at the end, that penetrated the blinds from the street outside and slewed across the ceiling of our bedroom. In our first weeks of living together, we had imagined all the things that smear of light might be: a dragon, a compressed Milky Way, an unfurling wave, an unwinding roll of toilet paper. These conversations usually occurred, as this one was occurring, after sex. Karolina and I defined our living together by our sleeping together. Our relationship had begun one night when we met for dessert at a diner in the Byward Market. As the diner was closing and the waiters were swabbing the tables, Karolina, concluding an account of the grating interpersonal dynamics among her housemates, said: "I'm just not willing to make the effort to be nice all the time. Why should I? I swear, from now on, I'm only living with people I'm in love with."

I could not reply. The longer I hesitated, the more piercing the tension grew. As soon as I laid my hand on her shoulder, we began kissing across the steel-rimmed table. Two months later we moved in together. We had been living together for six months: a fitful, fractious life driven by the insecurity of my short-term contracts with the federal government, the pressure of Karolina's translation program at the University of Ottawa, the lack of breathing space in our cramped, almost unaffordable apartment. Underlying these tensions was our peculiar pact that dictated we could not be less than certifiably, passionately ecstatic in one another's company. The demands we made meant that we were often disappointed with each other, and through each other, with ourselves. Our relations were unpredictable. Emotions did not develop so much as break off and turn into other emotions: exhaustion turned to disillusionment, nervousness turned to anger, irascibility turned to passion. Most of our conversations took place in bed, staring at the unfathomable shape on the ceiling.

"It's all so pretentious." Karolina straightened her body under the covers in a way that drew our hands and hips apart.

"Rich English people sipping tea ...! My grandparents were penniless immigrants."

"That's what I'm talking about — being an immigrant. That's what I am. Unlike you, who were born in Canada."

"Bart, I was born in a little town on Lake Superior. My dad was a lumberjack until he saved enough money to start his contracting business. My grandparents were almost illiterate. I don't know what they did back in the old country — the Irish ones or the Polish ones. But they sure weren't in a position to stop any wars. They were probably cannon-fodder."

I glanced across at the shadow of her arrestingly sharp chin, a perpetual surprise beneath the doughiness of her cheeks. She was staring at the ceiling. "Sorry," I murmured. "I just get fed up with people telling me I'm not an immigrant because I'm white and my parents speak English. I've got all the same immigrant compl — "

"It's not like you're from Ethiopia."

Karolina's lips pursed. I sensed she was fighting something: fighting the pain of the griping ordinariness of our conversation, the hurt of knowing that frustration and boredom were doomed to tatter our perfect passion. I stifled my retort that, though many people had to deal with both, confronting racism and coping with migrant dislocation were separate problems. I lay still, tenser than I had been the night when we had got together in the Market, with a cold tension that made me feel ugly. I waited for Karolina to speak.

She swallowed. "What were you going to tell me about this guy?"

"How little I know about him, mainly." He was no more than a face in Aunt Philippa's photographs. Or that was all he had been, until she began to tell me the story. The face looked too narrow to achieve the ruddiness boasted by most of the other male faces in the photos, the body too slight to aspire to first-rate sporting results. The pincer-like jut of my great-grandfather's nose, downturned at the end like the beak of an osprey, was rumoured to be a vestige of French ancestry. His unfashionably florid white mustache accentuated his foreignness. His name was an anglicization of the French surname Chenevert. Though no one could trace the precise link to France, Aunt Philippa's childhood memories included aged matrons speaking French to each other as they stooped down the corridors of the mansion in Bromley. In all the photographs I had seen, my great-grandfather's hair was white. "He was a redhead when he was young," Aunt Philippa said. "But he had a terrible shock and his hair turned white prematurely."

"What sort of shock?" I asked.

"The Great War," Aunt Philippa said. "The first one — 1914. He was a Congregationalist, you know. Severe low church people who believed in improving society. He worked for the London Missionary Society in Lambeth, coaching football for underprivileged boys. Nearly all the young men he trained died in the trenches. Year by year he watched them develop into formidable footballers, top of their form. Then they got sent off to France and in six months they were dead. Only one or two came back. He vowed he would never let that happen again."

He had a reputation for keeping his word. As a young man he had gone into the City to work for Lloyd's of London. One of his first acts was to insure a freighter that sank with all hands and a valuable cargo. He was young, only moderately well off, and he had to make an enormous pay-out. Other Lloyd's Names, in similar circumstances, went to court to deny their obligations. My great-grandfather paid up without a second thought. He sold most of his property to do it. "He was just starting a family," Aunt Philippa said. "I do not know how he managed it. But it wouldn't have occurred to him to act otherwise. And it made his name — made his name as a Name," she said with a giggle.

He earned a reputation for Congregationalist rectitude. It propelled him onto the Lloyd's board of directors. By the beginning of the Great War he was able to buy the Rolls Royce and hire Simmonds to drive it. He used his position to pursue his other interests. He became a Councillor of the British Football Association and President of the Amateur Football Alliance. He served as a magistrate for the County of Kent and was twice elected mayor of Bromley. Known by his initials, ABC, he argued on the side of practicality and good sense. When the King created him a Baronet, he chose as the motto for the family shield *Keep Straight On.*

"Where did they get the energy?" Karolina said. "I feel like I've had a good day if I go to a seminar, spend a couple of hours in the library and do a little work on one of my translation contracts." She frowned at the ceiling. "I bet it was all sublimination. I bet they didn't have sex."

"If he hadn't had sex I wouldn't be here," I said. "And as for work, don't forget they had servants and nannies."

"And bored stay-at-home wives."

"What's that supposed to mean?"

Karolina laid her palm on my thigh. "All right," she murmured. "Tell me the rest of the story."

⌒◦⌒

The Rhine was a flat-looking river. The stream of barges carrying coal and wooden crates whose contents it was better not to ask about made the current look still more placid. Mr. Chenvret knew that the Rhine was a long and important river, but to his mind it couldn't hold a candle to the bustling Thames. He stood next to his host, Dr. Bauwens, pretending to admire the river's flatness. In Germany every chap in a position of authority seemed to be Doktor-something-or-other, as though he were able to cure your ills. Most of them weren't medical men at all, simply chaps who talked a lot of bluster about philosophy and poetry. That was how Germany had got itself into its present state. If the Germans had put their noses to the grindstone and done a job of work rebuilding their country at the end of the Great War, they wouldn't have needed Herr Hitler to make the trains run on time.

Dr. Bauwens was a tall, fair man, with the intensely pale-skinned, almost Dutch look Mr. Chenvret had spotted here and there during his first hours in Cologne. The hair on the top of Dr. Bauwens's head had turned to thin grey wisps. He held himself upright with a pride of bearing that Mr. Chenvret found admirable, bordering on a rigidity that struck him as repellently Teutonic. Dr. Bauwens' English, though awkward, was comprehensible. This was a great relief, as it meant that one could talk to Dr. Bauwens without excessive interference from Gudrun, his large-boned, rather mannish daughter, who had lost no time in informing Mr. Chenvret that, having lived for a year in Swansea, she understood English people and their language perfectly. Swansea! What had she learned about the English in Swansea, from a pack of yelping Welshmen?

"I am jolly glad we found each other, Dr. Bauwens." As they walked back from the bank of the Rhine, Mr. Chenvret stared at the swastika-emblazoned red banners flying around the edges of the train station. He swung his cane. He carried it more as an embellishment than a support. "If young men are not given the healthy example of sport to occupy them, they will occupy themselves in war, and that will be disastrous for both our nations."

"Young men fight the war, Mr. Chenvret. But it is old men like us who make the war. We must show the old men in our countries that young men must do sport, not war."

"Since this spring, when Herr Hitler rescinded the Naval Agreement between our countries, I have been in a state of utmost despair. I am nearly seventy, Dr. Bauwens. In two years' time I will have had my three-score-years-and-ten. But I simply cannot sit still while England and Germany once again prepare to kill each other's young men. We have come too far for such barbarism."

Dr. Bauwens paused in mid-stride, his pale eyes closing against the breeze flailing off the Rhine. "The only true victory for either of our nations is the victory of sport over politics!"

"Now, Mr. Chenvret," Gudrun said. "Now we will visit the cathedral. One must see Cologne Cathedral! It is bigger than your cathedral at Westminster."

How German! Even the house of God was to be judged by the size of its mansions. Mr. Chenvret fancied he saw Dr. Bauwens wince at his daughter's words. There was no gainsaying the cathedral's massiveness, the enormous twin towers resembling gargantuan arms flung skyward in supplication. Though this part of Germany was Catholic, and in general Mr. Chenvret did not approve of popery, he consented to enter the building. Hadn't the Catholic Church's resistance to Herr Hitler increased since the Pope had issued his encyclical the year before last? The enemy of my enemy is my friend, he thought, staring heavenwards.

How he did wish that awful Gudrun would stop chattering!

"In this cathedral you will see all of Europe. You must not think of us as German, Mr. Chenvret. You must not think our Führer means ill towards Europe — "

"My daughter believes that we are two foolish old men," Dr. Bauwens said. "She does not think that there will be a war."

"We are Europeans," Gudrun said, "Look at the cathedral's lines. It is a blend of the cathedrals of Reims and Paris . . . similar to cathedrals in Italy . . . on a spot first excavated by the Romans, to whom Cologne was a colony: *Colonia* . . . And there you see the image of the Madonna of Milan — "

Milan, Mr. Chenvret thought. Italy . . . Oh, bother all this detail! It was all so tiresomely German. In the gloom of the transept, Mr. Chenvret's head spun. He steadied himself against a pillar. Edging forward a step, he found himself trapped in a column of pallid light. He squinted and noticed that Dr. Bauwens was squinting, also.

"Mr. Chenvret," Dr. Bauwens said. "Are you *gesund*? I have not noticed it before, but I hope you will not mind if I will say that your face . . . your face looks like the face of a man who has had a . . . a *Herzinfarkt*."

"A stroke," his daughter said, stepping forward in accusation.

"My heart is perfectly sound. My face is afflicted by Bell's palsy. My colleagues and family find this distracting. That is why I have grown this mustache. I would not have grown it otherwise. Do you think I would choose to look like a foreigner?"

"Here in the Rhineland," Dr. Bauwens said, "your mustache makes you look less foreign — "

"And in Italy it will make me look like a native! I have been thinking, Dr. Bauwens. We must do more! A single match here in Cologne will demonstrate our sporting spirit, but we must carry our campaign farther. Time is short. It is now July. The Great War began in autumn, and I fear the next war may do as well — unless we can stop it! Now that Herr Hitler and Mr. Mussolini have made their odious Pact of Steel, we must persuade the Italians, also, of the superiority of the sporting spirit to the war-like one. We must show Italy Englishmen and Germans playing football according to the rules of good sportsmanship. Together we can prove what rubbish all this talk is of nation turning against nation." He felt his voice rasping, and noticed faces below the altar staring in near-alarm at the flood of his forthright English. He caught his breath. "My lads are arriving tomorrow. They're a resilient side. If I tell them we're going on to Italy, they'll leap at the chance. What do you say, Dr. Bauwens? Will you collaborate with me in this?"

"I say, Mr. Chenvret, that you are a man of great conviction."

His descendants went on in the same pattern: working in business, organizing sports teams, devoting time to their churches. But no member of the family today trains the poor in the slums of East London. After the Second World War, the family's political allegiances migrated from the Liberal Party to the Conservatives. They abandoned the austere Congregationalist Union for the pomp of the Church of England. They began to think of themselves as people of importance in a way he probably never did. Would he find his descendants immoral? Even among my cousins, few married in youth, almost none had children born nine months after their wedding nights. What would A.B. Chenvret, Baronet, have made of me, a colonial too introverted to demonstrate the simple-minded exuberance the English expect of colonials? What would he have made of a fractured career, serial monogamy, long hair, terminal waywardness? Unreachable as his world — the world of Aunt Philippa's youth — has become, I cannot dispense with parts of his legacy.

The night I came home from work and told Karolina about my suspicion that the feasibility study I was working on was being skewed by politicos from the Prime Minister's Office to prod the civil servants towards the conclusion that the ideal site for a certain expensive boondoggle was in the middle of the Minister's riding, she said: "Don't worry about it, Bart. Just do your job."

"But, Karolina, if something's wrong you've got to say it's wrong."

"Jesus, you sound English! No normal immigrant would say a thing like that. Normal immigrants keep their heads down and make good in this country. Just because your family thinks it owns the place you figure you have the right to these principles — "

I walked out of the apartment, took the elevator down to the street and prowled through Lower Town. A silver church spire prodded the low sky, the Gatineau Hills skulked on the horizon. With nasal French ringing in my ears, I decided I had no choice. I would not be able to look at myself in the mirror if I let this pass. It did not matter where this conviction came from: it only mattered that I respect it. I went home and wrote a letter to my boss, outlining my concerns and the evidence suggesting political interference in our project. The next day I was transferred to a job collating the study's conclusions, a stultifying chore that cut off my access to raw data. A month later, when the contract ended, my boss made clear to me that I would not be hired to work on the Ministry's next project.

"What are you going to do now?" Karolina asked, staring at the ceiling. I had delayed telling her when I came in from work. After supper we had cleaned up, started to watch a video, then turned it off and gone to bed. Hard as a gallstone, the unannounced news swelled the pit of our pained lovemaking. The moment Karolina returned to bed from the bathroom, I told her.

"How can you just throw away your job?" she said. "Where are you going to find another one?"

"I had to do the right thing."

"Whatever you did, the main thing now is to get another job."

"Look at the light on the ceiling," I said. "It could be a searchlight. It could be London during the Blitz and the beams spreading out as they pick up the incoming bombers."

"It's not a searchlight," Karolina said, rolling over in bed to show me her shoulder. "It's not anything. It's just part of the crap you have to put up with when you live in a cheap apartment with old blinds and a streetlight outside the window."

My first glimpse of Cologne Cathedral was at night. I was on a train crossing Europe, oblivious of the route that would carry me from Ostend to Vienna. After my relationship with Karolina ended, I decided to leave Canada. Perhaps my parents' immigration had been a mistake: perhaps it wasn't destined to work out. When I was in university there had been no summer jobs, when I graduated from university the jobs I had got were short-term contracts, and now, as I turned thirty, the country was stifled by another recession. Europe, in the dazed afterglow of the fall of the Berlin Wall, offered expanding opportunities, cultural multiplicity, cresting optimism. My English birth now gave me the right to work in twelve countries. I flew to London, got a job as an office temp, went to parties with wild young Irish people taking London by storm and deranged New Zealanders hell-bent on enjoying every instant of licence before returning home. I stayed late enough at the parties to miss the last tube back across London and spend nights in narrow beds with drunken young women from Limerick and Christchurch who laughed out loud during sex and couldn't remember my name in the morning. At work the boss was always an Englishman; foreign temps, unlike British ones, did not become permanent employees. In contrast to the other foreigners, I understood English irony well enough to know when overseers were being rude to me. The other temps tolerated verbal abuse because they did not recognize it; I tried to retaliate. But, as I was not quite English enough to retaliate in an English way, my ripostes were judged crude, coarse — *colonial*. Fed up with London, I decided to travel east. Only as the train was speeding through Düsseldorf did I realize what was about to appear outside the window.

The Rhine glimmered black, streaks of white light zigzagging in the shuttling cradles of the wavelets. The glaring hull of the train station cast the surrounding district into blackness. Cologne Cathedral, enormous as a sculpted mountain, surged out of the darkness, blacker than the shadow engulfing it. Too huge to have been built by human hands, it shrank the old district of the city. Every passenger in the carriage remained glued to the window until we whooshed across the bridge, through the station and onwards in the direction of featureless Bonn. I thought of Aunt Philippa, clinging to her independence in her apartment. I thought of my great-grandfather's revelation that his only chance of inspiring peace was to take English and German soccer players to Italy.

I thought I would never see Cologne Cathedral again.

The train heaved on the mountainside. Big men in cheap jackets swarmed down the passageway. English and German footballers shared cigarettes as bow-tied Italian porters rushed to supply them with wine and *panini*. Gudrun flirted with the footballers by offering her services as interpreter. The phrases the Englishmen asked her to translate turned her broad face red beneath the low brim of her hat. Mr. Chenvret felt comfortably dwarfed by the frames of the large men crowding the swaying passageways. The footballers' good cheer filled him with a tenderness he could compare only to the emotions he had experienced when he had first been shown his daughters. Yet this present feeling was more invigorating than the poignancy inspired by fatherhood. These young men reminded him of the rough-edged Lambeth lads, born in the final months of the nineteenth century, who he had trained during the Great War — of all the men who had not survived to become husbands and fathers. "If we fail," he told McCready, the Fleet Street reporter sitting across from him, "these young men will go to war and many of them will die."

The Fleet Street fellow made a desultory gesture towards taking down his statement. He would ask his questions, then, likely as not, he would go away and print the grossest rubbish anyone could imagine. Your Fleet Street chap wasn't like your City man. He didn't have a sense of honour. It came from not having borne the trust of managing other people's money. Mr. Chenvret disliked speaking to men from the press. Now, though, he had no choice but to court such fellows. If his campaign was to have any effect, people must know about it.

Leaning towards McCready, Dr. Bauwens said: "Please tell the English people that the Germans believe in the sporting spirit also."

McCready stared at him from beneath the brow whose height was accentuated by his slicked-down, centre-parted hair. "How many Cup Finals can you remember, Mr. Chenvret?"

"More than fifty. The first one that's clear in my memory is the 1887 Cup, when Aston Villa beat West Bromwich Albion two-nil."

"Why does a man who is able to remember more than fifty Cup Finals," McCready said, "take an *amateur* side to represent England against the Boche? Surely you're inviting national humiliation?"

"Listen here, Mr. McCready, there's never humiliation in good sportsmanship. I asked the Football Association for a professional side and they refused, but I have no qualms about fielding a side of amateurs."

"Your amateurs will never be as good as professionals."

Mr. Chenvret averted his glance from the precipice falling away below the embankment. He glimpsed small houses with red tile roofs, a woman cooking at an outdoor stone oven amid dust and looping smoke. "In my young day," he said, fixing McCready with a stare, "football was played without a referee. Most of the professionals did a job of work during the week and did their training as well. Training today produces magnificent speed and fitness, but I'm not sure men aren't mollycoddled by massage and such like. Nowadays if a man gets a tap you'll see him rolling in agony. Then on comes the trainer with a sponge and a minute later he's running like a hare! Professional football has become marvellously mechanical . . . Now if a good amateur centre-forward, in the W.N. Cobbold tradition, ran down the field dribbling the ball instead of passing it, it might throw the mechanical defender out of his stride altogether. They don't dribble nowadays."

"Is that your strategy then? Dribbling?"

"Our strategy is to play a good ninety minutes of football. Amateurs are full of surprises. I'm proud to say I'm a bit of an amateur myself. No one expected me to do this."

McCready made a note in his jotter. "Four years ago Italy invaded Abyssinia. Now they are fighting in Albania and they may annex Tunisia. Herr Hitler, meanwhile, has broken his promise at Munich and absorbed Czechoslovakia. How can you justify consorting with such people?"

"I justify it in the same way I justify consorting with the press. I haven't any choice."

McCready's shoulders stiffened. "Are you saying you remain a proponent of appeasement?"

"I'm a proponent of good sportsmanship. Why must you always talk about politics?"

"I must talk about politics," McCready said, "because you have announced that your sporting tour has a political purpose: to prevent a war. This places you among the appeasers."

"I'm no appeaser, Mr. McCready. I am a man who, unlike you, is old enough to remember that watching young men compete is a sight better than watching them die. If we do go to war, you will be sitting in Fleet Street scribbling some sort of rubbish. But these lads," he said, waving in the direction of the carousing in the corridor, "will be out on the front lines being shot at."

"Thank you, Mr. Chenvret," McCready said, making a final note in his jotter. He shook hands with Mr. Chenvret, ignored Dr. Bauwens and left the compartment.

Dr. Bauwens slid away from the window. "My friend," he said, touching Mr. Chenvret's arm, "I think our job is very difficult."

❧

I met Gudrun in Italy. For five years I had been working in restaurants and teaching English as a Second Language. Whenever I saved some money I would skive away to spend a few weeks lounging on beaches on a Greek island or sitting at café tables in the old town square in Prague. Each time a job, a stash of bills or a relationship petered out, I picked up and moved on. Keep straight on. But my direction was always arbitrary. I would never be a member of a board, a mayor, a football coach; to become those things you needed to belong somewhere. I was not European and, on my rare visits back to Canada, I saw that Canadianness of the sort I had once possessed had been elbowed aside. Familiar commercial names had yielded to international chains, hockey teams I admired had moved to Colorado, everyone now understood obscurely American sports like basketball and, even in Ottawa, few people still worked for the government. My parents, who had been in Canada too long to return to Britain, had decided to stay. Aunt Philippa, now in her nineties, had been forced to leave her apartment for a seniors' home. I intended to visit her, but ran out of time. On the flight to Rome I could not sleep, berating myself for not having stayed the extra day.

My first glimpse of Gudrun made my body twitch with anxiety. She was in Italy on a kind of hippie holiday, revisiting the life she had lived a few years earlier when she had drunk her way around Europe with a succession of boyfriends. Walking on the beach at her side, I felt as enraptured as a child. The gold highlights in Gudrun's hair beneath the Italian sun, her long slender legs and incongruously broad shoulders riveted me. We tramped up and down the beach for two days, talking about movement and stasis, home and away, in a muddled mixture of English, German, French and Italian, before I smuggled her into the attic room above the hotel kitchen that came with my job. When our bodies arched together they grew as taut as two bows. Had I ever felt so staggered by sexual desire? So cascaded, depleted, engulfed by lust? We dozed and made love, dozed and made love, shuddering splay-legged at each inventive yoking of limbs and thighs like a pair of starfish seeking to form a pattern they know intuitively but cannot envisage. We could not keep our hands off each other. It bleared my eyes and bruised my lips. This kind of obsession wasn't supposed to happen after the age of thirty. But I was caught: at the end of the week I quit my job and followed Gudrun north.

Like other thirty-year-old Germans I had met, Gudrun was enmeshed in a shapeless, unfinishable Magister degree that involved studying a wide range of subjects in intimidating depth. She had to return to Germany for lectures. We took the train to Cologne and transferred underground to a subway that popped up out of the earth and became a streetcar skimming through the Ehrenfeld district with its Kurdish fugitives, Italian immigrants, left-wing eternal students and impoverished Eastern European refugees. In the alleys leading to the bars where Gudrun had got drunk after her last boyfriend had left, freshly damp posters were plastered on the walls each time a journalist was assassinated in Istanbul. Red slogans urged us to read the outlawed far-left German newspaper *Radikal*. Musicians in embroidered shirts strummed balalaikas on the street corners; there were red-paved bicycle paths, specialist bakeries, newspapers in half a dozen languages, stately Jugendstil buildings and neat low-rise apartment blocks with white stucco fronts. I noticed none of it. For two months we barely left Gudrun's top-floor flat. When I sat down to read she would saunter past me, trailing her fingers over the front of my jeans, halt to lend her fingertips a firmer purchase; then, with a lopsided smile, she would brush her fingers backwards and forwards, until a few minutes later, my jeans tangled around my ankles, I would be thumping on the floor on my back like an expiring beast. We made love forwards and backwards and upsidedown and end-to-end. Our relationship was so physical that it annihilated our minds and personalities. We spoke in a private panlingual gibberish. We were not German or European or English or Canadian; we were flesh detached from time and place. "Stupid man," Gudrun said. "How can I go to lectures when I have you naked in my bed?" She would make fun of my name, which meant "beard" in German. "*Bart, warum hast du kein Bart?* If you grew a beard you would look like other men here in Ehrenfeld. Everyone wouldn't know I have a foreign man in my flat."

"No one knows you have a foreign man in your flat. I never go out. I'm always here naked."

Naked, I trailed from bedroom to bathroom to kitchen. A poster on Gudrun's bathroom door, featuring a painting of a hapless-looking helmeted weasel, was emblazoned with the legend *Soldaten sind Marder* — "Soldiers are martens." A few months earlier a man had been arrested for carrying a placard bearing the words *Soldaten sind Mörder* — "Soldiers are murderers" — a sentiment whose expression, fifty-one years after the end of the last war, remained a crime. All over Germany people had reacted to this arrest by denouncing soldiers as martens. Staring at the poster day after day, I began to emerge from my flesh-drugged blur into a tangible time and place.

One day I got out of bed and stared out the window across the city. We were far from the centre, yet on the lip of the horizon two familiar towers rose against the sky.

My God! I thought. Cologne Cathedral. I'm in Cologne. *Cologne.*

I had spotted the towers during my first days in the city, but had blocked out the realization that this was the same cathedral I had stared at from the train years before. Now we became sightseers. We scoured the streets of the old city, inside the road known as the *Ring*, that followed the arc of the ancient city walls. I felt as light-headed and unsure of my footing as a man returning to earth from a balloon ride. Only on the third day of our walking, talking (on the street we abandoned our gibberish for straightforward English or German), sitting in *Kneipes*, visiting museums or going to repertory cinemas, did I tell Gudrun about my great-grandfather.

"I knew it!" she said, pushing aside the slender glass of beer she was sipping. She laid her hands flat on the table of the underground bar. "You English people! You set foot in Germany and you have to talk about the war."

"But this is my family," I said, "my past . . . "

"Do you think my family does not have a past? My father's older brothers were killed by bombs when they were children, my mother was a refugee. But I don't think about these things. That is the past. We know it was bad, but now we live differently."

I felt my vehemence dissolve. Staring at Gudrun's black leather jacket and dishevelled hair, I saw that we had been cut loose by the same war. My parents, growing up in a shabby post-war England whose heroic self-image was deflated by crumbling row-houses and spartan rationing, had left for Canada as soon as they finished school. Gudrun and her long-haired, Green-voting, eternal student friends owed their opting out to a memory of what Germany had been like the last time that everyone had zealously opted in. A war that had ended more than fifty years earlier had vaulted both of us out of expected orbits. I was no longer British, she refused to think of herself as German. "I am a Rhinelander and I am a European!" she would reply, if I casually generalized about Germans. The difference was that I wanted to talk about it, while Gudrun, who felt that my talking was a way of blaming her for events that had occurred long before her birth, did not.

I decided to tell her about Dr. Bauwens.

"Ah," she said, "a good German!"

I faltered. "He had a daughter named Gudrun."

She smiled. "Gudruns are always special people."

"I know where he lived." I could remember the address from the embossed head of the yellowish, almost cardboard-like letter Aunt Philippa had shown me seven years earlier. *Dr. P.J. Bauwens. Köln A. Rh. 15 August 1939. Clever Strasse 13.*

"That's inside the Ring," Gudrun said. "On the northern edge of the old city, near the St. Kunibert church."

"So it's close? We can go and see it? Perhaps his family still lives there." I hesitated. Then, with a laugh, I said: "Perhaps we can meet the other Gudrun. By now, she must be about seventy-five."

Gudrun stared at me, her expression sheering from perplexity to a throttled fury. As I leaned forward in confusion, her fingers pegged my wrist to the table. "Don't you realize the whole old city is a reconstruction? Your lovely English bombers destroyed ninety-five per cent of it during the war. It has all been rebuilt. You dropped fourteen bombs on Cologne Cathedral. But the Cathedral survived. The rest of the old city was ... *Trümmer.*" She swallowed and pulled herself upright, adjusting her leather jacket on her shoulders.

"And Dr. Bauwens?" I mused aloud. "And Gudrun?"

"If they lived on Clever Strasse, they're probably dead. The British bombers killed nearly everybody who lived there."

Mr. Chenvret always felt at home on a football pitch. "Isn't it marvellous?" he said to McCready. "You can be in a place like Venice that is so utterly foreign, yet you step onto a football pitch and immediately you know how everything works. It's one of the great hopes for mankind."

They stood at the edge of the pitch, the reserves murmuring among themselves on the bench in front of them. Mr. Chenvret coughed. Their interminable tours of the canals of Venice had given him a chill. He felt exhausted, dispirited by the Blackshirts he had seen standing guard at the *vaporetto* stops. More than anything else, he felt old. His world had ended with the outbreak of the Great War. For the last twenty-five years he had understood less and less of how people thought and acted. But he knew he must keep on. Through his glasses he could discern Dr. Bauwens, pacing the grass on the opposite side of the pitch, shouting instructions to his lads.

"Are you going to biff the Boche today?" McCready asked.

"We're going to play a jolly good match of football," Mr. Chenvret said, feeling the hoarseness in his throat as he strained to make himself heard over the enormous, cheering crowd. After the match at Milan, he had decided that he liked Italian crowds. They did not seem to choose sides between Englishmen and Germans: they cheered any good run, any daring cross, any goal or act of bravado. They cheered out of pleasure, as an English crowd would rarely allow itself to cheer.

"You were lucky to come out of the match at Milan with a draw," McCready said.

"A good amateur side that really trains can hold its own for the first half against professionals because the professionals don't know what to expect. After that you have to be lucky."

Mr. Chenvret turned, following the play. "Move forward!" he shouted, his voice turning to a stammer against the howls of the crowd. "I want all five forwards on the attack!" He coughed, stumbled, poked out his cane. McCready was at his side. "In my young day you could tell where a man played because he kept his position. Nowadays the forwards feel they have to defend as well. It's a complete dog's breakfast! Let each man do his job!"

The forwards ran into the German defence. A cross trickled through, but the man who bolted in to pick it up was offside. The Italian referee moved the play back towards the centre of the pitch. Ineffectual crosses trickled off the edges of the pitch. The throw-ins were kicked high in the air, then headed back and forth. "You're not playing badminton!" Mr. Chenvret called. "It's *foot*ball, not head ball."

When the whistle blew, ending the first half, the ball was high in the air above the middle part of the pitch, and the teams were tied nil-nil.

During halftime, Mr. Chenvret told his lads to keep the ball on the ground. "Dribble! Take some good long runs. The spectators will enjoy it and the other side won't expect it. They expect you to pass and they expect you to play the ball in the air. So do the opposite. And always play as sportsmen. It'll be smashing if we win today, but win or lose we must be able to tell ourselves that we played the game as it's meant to be played."

Before the whistle blew to open the second half, Dr. Bauwens walked to the middle of the pitch. He waved, and Mr. Chenvret, coughing, stumped out to join him. The view from the middle of the pitch made him gasp. It was years since he had seen a large stadium from this angle: the perfect symmetry of the grass sweeping away, the goals at either end of the pitch looking as small and precise as croquet hoops. Flags beat back and forth in the stands: Italian tricolours, German eagles, one flag bearing a swastika and two beleaguered Union Jacks. He saw rank upon rank of men standing and cheering. Someone was blowing a horn. Mr. Chenvret wondered whether they would all be able to come back here in a year's time. "Thank you," he murmured under his breath. "Thank you. Thank you."

Dr. Bauwens extended his hand. Mr. Chenvret, transferring his cane to his left hand, shook it. The crowd howled. The players stood rooted on the turf, observing the shrieking crowds. The referee stepped forward, paused before the numbing, thunderous ovation, then motioned for play to resume.

Mr. Chenvret walked back to the edge of the pitch. When he reached the bench, he seated himself next to the reserves. His breath was heaving in his chest.

"You wouldn't catch me shaking hands with the Hun," McCready said.

Mr. Chenvret followed the play. When the players lunged past he could feel the impact of their heels in the earth sending tremors up his cane. He could hear their rasping breaths and stifled oaths and see the black patches of sweat gaping like wounds on their jerseys. The truth was, his lads were knackered. They weren't used to playing powerful professional sides. And most had never before been abroad: the long train journeys, the strange food, the oddity of foreign hotels, the persistent nagging of the pressmen, were taking their toll. By the twentieth minute of the second half they were lagging one step behind Dr. Bauwens's men. The German centre-forward took a pass, accelerated around a floundering English defender and rattled a shot off the crossbar while the goalkeeper stood paralysed.

The crowd moaned.

"They nearly had you there," McCready said.

"It is trying how slow the game becomes when players are tired. In my young day there was more charging. I remember Lord Kinnaird looking over his red beard at the beginning of a match and saying, 'Shall we kick or hack today?'" Mr. Chenvret chuckled. The cough caught him and bent him forward. He sat down on the bench. "Of course I don't want kicking or hacking. Don't put that in your awful paper, McCready. But players then were hard. Referees allowed a good hard charge without penalizing it. The game moved more quickly because of it."

By the thirty-eighth minute play was mired in the English end. A defender and an attacker collided; the ball sprang into the air. The crowd uttered a howl. Players from both teams swarmed in close to the English goal. As the ball descended an English player launched himself skyward and knocked it clear with his head. The ball looped down towards the German centre-half, who kicked it on the fly, driving a waist-high shot into the tumult of men in front of the goal. The ball ricocheted into the corner of the English net, while a German player crumpled as though shot, sucked his fist in pain, then rushed to join his celebrating comrades.

"Hand ball!" Mr. Chenvret shouted. "It went in off his hand."

"They're not going to allow it!" McCready said. "They simply can't do such a thing!"

The English players had surrounded the referee. He looked around in bewilderment.

The crowd's applause had turned to a shuddering, seesawing sound.

"It's a bloody conspiracy!" McCready bellowed. His hat had slipped back on his head. His fists were clenched.

"The referee was blocked by the play," Mr. Chenvret said. "He couldn't see it."

The referee stepped clear of the melee. Facing first one side of the stadium then the other, he signalled a goal.

The crowd howled like a creature being ripped open. Furious, exultant applause rocked against a mounting wave of boos, hisses and imprecations. The Blackshirts in the corners of the stadium paced out their rounds.

"It's a bloody scandal!" McCready shrieked. "Mussolini and Hitler ganging up on John Bull! It's not fair cricket that. I'm telling you, Mr. Chenvret, that's just what was done to Neville Chamberlain at Munich. 'I have your piece of paper.' Well that's all it is — a bloody piece of paper! The Eyties and the Boche will cheat you every time. If they can't beat you fair and square, they'll beat you with a crooked referee. The only rule these people understand is the rule of the gun, and the sooner everyone in England realizes that the bloodywell better!"

"Mr. McCready, please use more temperate language. And please think of the consequences before you write an inflammatory article. Don't poison sport with your politics."

"But Mr. Chenvret, my readers *expect* politics in their sport. I'm only giving them what they want. Just like you I have a job of work to do."

McCready walked away.

On the field, the English players had regrouped and were making runs down the edges of the pitch. Good hard runs, Mr. Chenvret thought; impressive runs for men who were dispirited and fatigued. With seven minutes left to play there was little hope, but they kept straight on. They ran themselves to exhaustion until the referee blew the final whistle.

The crowd rose to its feet and gave the teams a standing ovation.

That evening, on the train that would carry the players and pressmen back to Cologne, Mr. Chenvret, Dr. Bauwens and Gudrun sat alone in a closed compartment. Mr. Chenvret overheard the English pressmen discussing the evidence of Italian and German turpitude. The German and English footballers stood in the passageway sharing cigarettes, but their conversation was subdued. None of the Englishmen invited Gudrun to translate for them.

⁓

The story that began with an old woman ended with an old man.

During the Second World War my great-grandfather lost his memory. He remembered the London Missionary Society, the Lambeth lads who died in the trenches in the Great War; he remembered that he worked at Lloyd's of London, and he remembered the names of famous footballers from before the Great War — W.N. Cobbold, G.O. Smith, A.M. Walters and his brother P.M. Walters — but he forgot that in July and August 1939, he had tried to prevent the outbreak of the Second World War. He did not remember that his tour had backfired, intensifying mistrust and hysteria in all three countries when British journalists seized on a bad goal as a propaganda tool. He retired into long-standing routines — routines that persisted after the end of the war that he had been unable to prevent. Until shortly before his death in 1950 he would get up in the morning, dress in a suit, eat a light breakfast and walk out to the Rolls Royce. He sat down in the back seat, draping himself in the dark blue rug he kept in the car. Simmonds drove him into the City, drove him home again for lunch, then drove him back into the City in the afternoon and home again in the evening. He retained an office at Lloyd's and was tolerated by the staff, though everyone knew he was senile and could no longer attend board meetings. My mother, then a little girl, was told that when she went to lunch with Grandfather Chenvret at the mansion in Bromley she could invite a friend, but she must choose someone who did not mind being asked seven times during lunch: "So, my dear, what is *your* name?"

When my great-grandfather returned to England from his tour of Germany and Italy, the press gave him a rough ride. He put his head down, refusing to apologize for subjecting English footballers to "humiliation" by the propaganda armies of Mussolini and Hitler, refusing to reply to questions or taunts. Dr. Bauwens wrote him a letter at his club in Bromley.

Dear Mr. Chenvret,

The photo enclosed, made by my daughter at Venice, may you remember also the matches at Köln and Milano, and the glorious match at Venice, where the players and the crowd were nothing else as sportsmen and did not care about political tensions. It was a great victory of sport over politics. And when your players accepted a doubtful goal in a good attitude they gave a wonderful example of discipline, a better one than some of your pressmen.

With my best wishes, yours very sincerely,

Dr. P.J. Bauwens

I inherited the photograph, like the letter, after Aunt Philippa's death. They were in the bottom of the engraved box whose lid I had watched her open. The photograph depicts a group of middle-aged men in dark suits and jackets and wide, boldly patterned ties standing on the broad steps projecting out from a narrow doorway. The word *"ristorante"* is affixed to the glass panel above the door; lozenges of cross-hatched latticework, fronted by semi-tropical plants in large pots, frame the steps. The men have the comfortably stout look that men used to acquire in their middle years, before middle-aged men were divided between the aerobicized and the obese. My great-grandfather stands front and centre, his white mustache formidable. He is older and slenderer than the other men; he clutches his cane like a rapier. His expression is more fixed than the easy smiles of the Italian-looking men and the jolly smiles of the ones I take to be the Germans. Only his family, and Dr. Bauwens, knew that Mr. Chenvret owed his English stiffness to Bell's palsy.

I stare and stare at the photograph, but I will never know which of the men is Dr. Bauwens, just as I will never know whether my great-grandfather replied to this letter during the two weeks that remained before the outbreak of war. I will never know what Gudrun looked like. One day, when I was still living in Cologne, I walked to Clever Strasse and found a building with the number 13/15. It was a post-1945 redbrick office building with brown blinds in the windows, occupied by a company that described itself as a *Kapitalanlagegesellschaft* — an investment brokerage. In the Cologne city archives the other Gudrun later discovered the names of Dr. Bauwens and the first Gudrun among the victims of the British bombing raid that had destroyed the original building at Clever Strasse 13. When I received her letter in Ottawa, I remembered how, after she released my wrist from the table of the basement bar in the reconstructed old city inside the Ring, we had walked to Cologne Cathedral and climbed the five hundred steep stone steps rising into the heavens. When we came out onto the narrow, wiremesh-enclosed walkway of the observation area, the sky had smeared to a creamy white haze infected by the industrial residues of nearby Leverkusen. The dense yellowish clouds combed into the colourless background might have been camouflaged missiles, children wriggling towards life, ancient castles dissolving to filmy dust. All around us, large black-and-white photographs showed what this view had looked like in 1945. The old city had been pulverized, smashed flat by the bombing. Nothing from that time could have survived.

History intruded more and more on Gudrun and me, flooding Gudrun's top-floor flat in Ehrenfeld the way that daylight floods through the curtains when the lovers must part at dawn. Our coupling bodies could not remain eternally innocent. The strangeness of our being together, the disparities between our points of reference — what could she know about Ottawa? What could I understand about growing up in the Rhineland? — cranked us into a state of greater and greater tension. Merely being in the same room felt unnatural. By the end of my third month in Ehrenfeld she asked me to leave.

I returned to Canada, hoping for the first time in years to be able to stay. The longing was as insistent as it was irrational. Eager to heal the rifts in my past, I found the address of Karolina's translation business in the Yellow Pages and phoned her. "You remember that story about my great-grandfather? The one who tried to stop the war? I know the rest of it now."

"I'm married, Bart. I'm the mother of a three-year-old girl. Your great-grandfather doesn't interest me. Tell your story to yourself."

I put down the receiver. Aunt Philippa had died two weeks earlier. My friends from school and work had scattered. The past had swallowed my future. Ottawa's neo-Gothic spires, gloomily and more nordically reminiscent of their European Gothic prototypes, planted Cologne Cathedral at the core of my mind's eye. I learned from my parents that, even after moving into the seniors' home, Aunt Philippa had maintained the apartment off Sparks Street. She had been unable to admit to herself that she would never return to that nook where her memories had flourished, just as her father, at the end, clung to the names and deeds of pre-1914 footballers. My parents suggested that, as a downtown base would make job-hunting easier, I should consider moving into Aunt Philippa's apartment. Her investment portfolio, sustained by the remains of her father's earnings at Lloyd's and her husband's earnings at Dunlop, would continue to pay the rent until the end of the lease. Like a usurer living off ancient revenues, I crept downtown. I headed towards the Marks and Spencer on Sparks Street to buy oatcakes, shortbread and long grey socks. But Marks and Spencer, a sign on the door informed me, had left Canada. I stared through the locked glass doors at empty shelves and bare counters. A tilting sign advertised a going-out-of-business sale. I tested the doorhandle: the door was locked. I looked for a few moments then continued towards the apartment, relieved that Aunt Philippa had not lived to see the end of the story.

MISS WHY

MY FATHER TOLD me secrets when he chopped wood. "Why?" I asked him. "Why are things like this?"

"Come outside," he said. "We need firewood."

"Agnieszka," my mother said, "it is bad to ask so many questions."

My father preferred to tease me. Miss Why, he called me. *Pani Dlaczego*. But once we were out of the house he would try to answer my questions. In the city a man like him might suspect that his flat had been bugged, but there was little danger of this in our village. It was my mother, not the secret police, my father was evading. My mother believed in not endangering children, my father believed in not lying to them. When I asked questions, their beliefs collided.

My mother had little cause for worry. Stone walls rising to the height of my father's chest enclosed our yard. Beyond our front gate and the wide verge of tall grass, the dirt road leading through the village struck out into the countryside. Farmers in horsedrawn carts waved to my father as they jolted past.

In their yards our neighbours scattered feed for their chickens and repaired the small arbours where their flowers grew. My father spoke into his chest in a mumble that the squawking of chickens, the splintering crack of axe on wood, the hissing of a goose or the barking of a dog made inaudible to the neighbours, and nearly to me as well. "Why?" I would ask. "Why is there no meat in the village? Why does the priest say the general is a bad man? Why do things cost so much? Why are the steel workers marching in Gdańsk . . . ?" My father's mumbles grew longer and more complicated as my questions became more impassioned.

My mother was afraid I would repeat the things my father told me to my friends, who would repeat them to their parents. But I knew better than that. My reticence had nothing to do with politics: it came from being different. We were a strange family, my mother, my father, my little brother and I. We lived in a village, but we were not peasants. My father was a Magister from the University of Katowice. When I was ten he became director of our regional secondary school. Once, when I was very young, my father had gone to work in West Germany for six months. In addition to the Deutschmarks other men brought back, he returned speaking and reading good German. For a few years, well-dressed Germans drove out to our village in the summer to visit him. My friends could not imagine having such a father. "Aren't you afraid of him?" they would ask. I did not reply. I knew I could say nothing of how we lived at home: the books we read, the educated vocabulary we used around the supper table — it all made us stranger. My father's criticisms of our socialist government were only a tiny part of the oddness I had to keep secret if I wished to be friends with the girls at school. I wanted to know why things happened, but once I had answers I kept them to myself and turned them over in my mind, testing them against the life I saw around me in the shops along the shaded dirt street and the swooping yellow fields of rapeseed awaiting the harvest. I was fifteen when the change came: *die Wende,* as they say here in Germany. Our new government told us we must draw "a thick line" under our past. I do not wish to be critical of my contemporaries, but when I left the village and travelled the 150 kilometres to Katowice to the university, I discovered that most students knew little about our history. They knew that things used to be worse, but all they thought about was which clothes or shoes they could buy, and whether they could afford a shopping trip to Frankfurt that year. I don't mean to say I had no friends. I was like other students: I drank beer and I went to discos. I loved to dance all night, inventing new shapes from myself with a writhe, or a toss of my long hair, feeling my strong, lean body outlined against the strobe in a pose no one else could have struck because no one else had ever been who I was at that moment. But my life was elsewhere. As I saw my classmates marrying — many of them becoming parents at twenty-one, just as young people had under the old system — I realized that this was not going to happen to me. My exclusion did not surprise me. It came, I saw, from my family's habit of apartness. As in the village, I was friends with other students in a way that excluded confiding in them. Secrets were a commodity I could not imagine sharing. Studying business management, I learned to think of that which could be exchanged as bearing a price. Trading away my secrets would exact a cost. Regardless of the intimacies I gained in return, I sensed that giving others my secrets would result in a loss.

In the holidays I returned to the village, where the mothers of the girls I had gone to school with told me about their daughters' weddings. My father continued to speak into his chest when he chopped wood: the new government had disappointed him. Fewer peasants passed on their carts now, and those who did rarely waved. "They're forced to sell their crops for nothing," my father said. The peasants wanted the socialist government back: at least then they had been able to earn a living. "These are ignorant people," my father said. "The government should look after them better. One has to recognize that people like that will never adjust to this new world. Not like you, Agnieszka. You're an educated girl. You'll get your Magister in a subject that didn't exist when I was in university. Everything we fought for will be yours."

The more often my father repeated these words, the more sorry I felt for him. Being director of the regional secondary school was less important than it had been when education was respected. The most esteemed man in the area now was a doctor who had stolen equipment from a state hospital to set up a private medical clinic, then used his profits to bring an American burger franchise to a nearby large town. My father hated these changes, and he hated the peasants for making him feel as backward as they were.

When I returned to Katowice, I went into an internship arranged by my professor. I sat in the office of a factory and watched ordinary people try to solve problems that were either very simple, such as which side of the warehouse trucks should park on, or completely insoluble, such as the absence of a market for the mining equipment the factory produced. This experience was supposed to provide me with the data to write my Magister thesis. I believe in hard work, and I always do what I must, but finishing my Magister thesis was very difficult. I could see that the factory would soon close; my thesis felt like a post-mortem report. My flat-mates wished to talk only about shoes and clothes and shops in Frankfurt or Berlin. When they went out with their boyfriends they dressed almost as badly as Russian women. I thought of my father's years of resistance to the Russians. How ashamed he would be to see Polish university students wearing such awful dresses and so much makeup! One afternoon one of my flat-mates returned with a man who was thirty-two years old. She left him in the kitchen while she went to dress, and we began to talk. Adam's whole upbringing had taken place under socialism. He had been twenty-three and preparing to write his Magister thesis before the study of Marxism-Leninism was removed from the university curriculum.

"Don't you find students today superficial?" I asked. I thought I had offended him, insulting his choice of my flat-mate as a girlfriend. But he smiled from the hollows beneath his eyes. He began to describe the debates he had had with his university friends about the form of future Polish society. "Are you sure you want to hear about this?" he asked, glancing in the direction of the bedroom my flat-mate and I shared.

"Yes," I said, lifting my chin to examine his weary eyes. Adam told me about the demonstrations he had marched in, his first girlfriend, who had dyed her hair and worn punk clothes, how exciting life had been, how everyone had aligned himself with a party or a dissident organization or a splinter group; how they had felt themselves sliding across the cusp of history, knowing that soon the Russians would be gone and Poles would be in control to make their history as they pleased.

"But that's not what happened," I said.

"Things are improving," he said, shrugging his shoulders. "Prices are too high and wages are too low, but — "

"But things mean nothing."

The door opened and my flat-mate came out of our room looking like the whore of a Russian Mafia king. Adam looked at me and I looked at him, and we both knew.

A week after defending my Magister thesis I ran away to Germany with Adam. There was nowhere else to go. The West was inside us; we could complete ourselves only by living there. My parents were not as angry as I had feared. My father, accustomed to feeling outraged and bewildered, was beyond disillusionment. My mother told us to get married in the first church we passed, but behind her admonishments I could hear her relief that I had a man at last, a man who was older and would look after me. She would have preferred that I marry at twenty, rather than waiting until the age of twenty-four to do something like this, but for her the important consideration was that I would be protected. And me? I didn't care what anybody thought. I cared least of all what a priest might think. The priests were so powerful before the world changed — *vor der Wende*, as the Germans say — when every Polish priest was a political prophet. Now people are tired of them. All a priest can do is tell you not to kiss before you get married. What nonsense! Here in Germany I can't enter a Catholic church without seeing some young Polish woman dropping to her knees in prayer. But I can tell you that most of those devout young women aren't the virgins the priests would wish them to be. You can't spend your weekends in discos all through university and live the way a priest expects. That's why I rarely enter the churches here, and when I do I admire the paintings and the architecture, and refuse to cross myself. Perhaps by doing this, I have become as cut off from myself as those girls who think only about shopping and shoes and makeup; perhaps, like them, I had little choice.

Why not? Couldn't my life have turned out differently? I work changing sheets in a hotel in the Rhineland. Adam works in a restaurant. They're immigrant jobs: jobs for Turkish peasants, not educated Europeans like us. But I don't believe my life would have been different had I remained in Katowice. It's not just that the factory has closed — I might have found a good job, I might have moved to Warsaw and made money working for a German or American company. But a good job earning złotys is not much better than a bad job earning Deutschmarks. In Warsaw I would wear the same clothes and dance to the same music. The West is everywhere now, so why not live in a Western country? In the evening, when I go to my German classes, I see that much of Poland has reached the same conclusion. Three-quarters of my class is Polish. If we all stay here and have our children, Germany will become as mixed as Silesia, with Polish and German intermingled to the point where no one can say where one ends and the other begins. Poland, too, looks more mixed to me now. Last year, when Adam and I returned for a visit, listening to conversations in the streets made me realize that most of the Katowice dialect words that had amused me when I arrived in the city as a student were actually German words. I thought of my father resisting the Russians, of how I and my friends had sulked during Russian class in school: why hadn't we noticed that all the time we were slipping westward, as our country had slid westward across the map at the end of the last war?

I haven't stopped asking questions, though today you would have to call me *Frau Warum*. The Germans barely use *Fräulein* now, so every woman is *Frau*, just as in Poland every woman is *pani*. I'm caught in the same puzzle in both languages. By the time Adam and I have finished working and gone to our night classes we have little time to think about problems such as whether we will stay in Germany, or whether we will marry. Sometimes I start asking questions and we talk for half the night, but more often we go to bed early in order to be up for work in the morning. Work is where I do most of my thinking. As I toss sodden sheets and pillowcases into the revolving bins of the dryers in the hotel basement, I think of my father's time in Germany.

After he had been working in Hannover for six months, my father was given the chance to bring his family to live in the West. He came home to the village to make his decision. He and my mother talked late into the night, their voices keeping me and my brother awake. We shivered in our beds, wondering what school would be like in Hannover, whether the city had ice cream and trams. But, balanced against those pleasures, was my father's dignity in a world that had resisted the West. In Poland my father was a man of standing, a Magister, a person with responsibility for the education of the young. Why should he give that up to spend the rest of his life as a *Gastarbeiter*? "And the children," I heard him say to my mother, who thought we would live better in Hannover. "Deutschmarks cannot buy them a culture." For him it was clear-cut, like two pieces of wood split by the blade of an axe: you chose one life or the other, there were different lives to choose. Even now I wake at night thinking I've heard that two-stroke beat, the splinter and the thunk as the two pieces of wood fall away in opposite directions and the axe buries its head in the chopping-block. But usually it's just a motor scooter passing beneath the window, and in the morning, as I get up for work, I tell myself that no sound disturbed my sleep.

DUTY CALLS

Tibor stepped into the hall and wondered why he had come. The aisle dividing the pews, which had been remastered as leather-cushioned benches of parliamentary plushness, led towards a stage where a varnished podium awaited the speaker. Grey-haired men wearing crests on their blazers, their accents remotely British in a clipped Upper Westmount way, discussed people they had known since childhood and ancient political quarrels. "For my money," one man said, "René Lévesque was simply a traitor." Tibor could feel his jaw tightening.

Andy Johnson, an old McGill classmate, laid a hand on his shoulder. "Let me introduce you to Tibor," he said in a voice that seemed to have grown louder over the last fifteen years. "At McGill we called Tibor the Mad Hungarian."

Tibor shook hands with a lawyer from Andy's firm. "I knew your wife's parents," the lawyer said. "Their cottage in the Townships — "

Over the lawyer's shoulder Tibor spotted Jane. Jane Merton. They had worked together in a broker's office near Square

Victoria when he was starting out. They had run into each other over the years at meetings such as this one, then at some point she had disappeared — until three months ago, when he had spotted her at the corner of Sherbrooke Street, waving at him from amid a flock of homebound commuters streaming out of a bus to head down the slope towards the Peel Métro station. She looked blithe, almost girlish — younger than she had all those years ago in that dim office. Two years back, she told him, she had quit her job and gone travelling. She had worked in a hotel in the south of France, hooked up with another woman to share a cabin on a tramp steamer from Athens to Israel, and returned to Western Europe through Syria, Turkey and half a dozen other countries. The impulsiveness of it all had whirled around the inturned wings of her auburn hair as the commuters marched in lock-step towards the mouth of the Métro entrance.

"Was your family's cottage around there, too?" the lawyer was asking. "Was that how you and Sue met up?"

"My family's cottage was on Lake Balaton," Tibor said. "We lost it in 1956."

"Lake Balaton?" the lawyer said. "That's a new one on me. Is it close to Magog?"

"It's in Hungary." Andy, who must recall similar scenes from McGill parties, spoke in a placating rush. "Tibor's parents were refugees from Communism."

Jane, wearing a fuchsia dress, was advancing up the aisle. Had she noticed him? He tried to remember what she had told him on Sherbrooke Street. Wasn't she living with a man — somewhere in Ville St-Laurent? Yes, now it came back: Jane's new boyfriend was a Lebanese businessman, a leading vendor of syrupy desserts to Middle Eastern restaurants in Montreal and Ottawa.

"Yeah, but your cottage here," the lawyer said. "Were you in the Laurentians? I don't remember anybody Hungarian in the Townships."

"My cottage," Tibor said, "was an East End triplex — four of us in three rooms. In the summer we opened the windows. That was our vacation."

He stepped out from between Andy and the lawyer, certain now that Jane had noticed him. The lawyer's assurance that immigrants were always welcome in this Anglo rights group ricocheted away over his shoulder.

"I didn't know you'd be here," Jane said.

"Where would this country be without immigrants?" the lawyer said. His voice dropped. "What did Sue's parents *think* . . . ?"

"I forgot to cancel my membership, so they sent me an invitation."

"And you came?" Jane's smile pulled her cheeks into flushed pouches. The bunched-up abundance of her face, her incongruously wide mouth and mildly upturned eyes, lent her a topsy-turvy expression. Her thick hair sparked with reddish licks he didn't remember having noticed before. Caught in her glow — could his presence have contributed to this radiance? — he felt unable to speak.

What made a woman look that good?

"She took the one-way ticket down the 401," Andy muttered. The lawyer responded with a grunt.

"I don't know why I came," Tibor said. "Habit, I guess. Duty."

"I'm glad you came."

They sat down on one of the long, cushioned benches. The cool fabric of her dress grazed his light cotton slacks. "I must be the only man here not wearing a tie." He tugged at the collar of his sports shirt. Lowering his voice, he said: "This place used to belong to the Catholic church. Just look at this room. It was obviously used for sermons. Sermons *in French*. Doesn't anybody think this is a little weird?"

"Not this crowd," Jane said.

"Ladies and gentlemen." An elderly man spoke into the microphone. "Please take your seats, ladies and gentlemen."

Andy, ambling past in conversation with the lawyer, arched his eyebrows in Tibor's direction. Tibor could imagine what they would murmur to each other once they were out of earshot: just what you'd expect from the Mad Hungarian — walking out on us to nab the one attractive woman in the room. Perhaps, Tibor thought, they should ask themselves why there was only one woman in her thirties here; why he, Jane and Andy were the youngest people in the crowd; why people in their twenties did not attend Anglo rights meetings.

The speaker, a man in his fifties, wore a pale silk tie that absorbed the dull afternoon light. His beige suit looked too tropical for Montreal on the brink of autumn. His thick grey hair was parted on one side with schoolboy scrupulousness. When he began to speak, his words emerged in a block-paragraph monotone that reminded Tibor that a few years earlier this man had published an unreadable book called *The Principle of Equality*.

" . . . A noble principle," he said. "A principle whose denial leads inexorably to the dissolution of democratic government. When we fight to save the English language, when we fight to include English words on signs, we are waging the noblest struggle of all — "

Jane grabbed his sleeve and made a face. Tibor observed the colour of her eyes, a dark hazel enlivened by the merest inlay of green.

" — the struggle for *democracy!*"

Tepid applause, a war-whoop from Andy and an ancient, English-sounding "Hear, hear" from one of the old men in blazers. Jane rolled her eyes. He leaned towards her. Mouthing the words more than speaking them, he said: "*Let's go.*"

Leaving unobtrusively was out of the question. They got to their feet and paraded down the aisle side by side in a hasty reverse wedding-march, past the frowning spectators and out the door. Their shoes clapped on the merciless hardwood. Tibor could hear a tiny, appalled hesitation interrupting the speaker's faultless diction. They pushed through the double doors and walked in silence down the long stone corridor leading out of the building.

"Did you see the looks on their faces?" Jane said, as their feet alighted on the front steps. The late August day had grown cool. A shower carrying a hint of a chill had slicked the trunks of the oaks and maples in the yard, coaxing an overripe glow from the grass. A prematurely orange leaf lay smeared on the path to the street. Overhead the trees at the summit of the dark Mountain had speared a white rag of mist. Jane laughed, throwing her arm around Tibor with a clumsy, giggling squeeze. "God, I'm never going back there!" She released him. They walked hip to hip towards the sidewalk with a briskness that ruled out his returning her squeeze. "I'm sitting there," she said, "and I'm thinking where do these people *live*? I had to go up to Trois-Rivières for work last week — my boss just bought this *entrepôt* up there. When I was driving back I realized I hadn't seen a single English sign all day and I hadn't even noticed. It's all the same to me now. I mean, there are things I'm willing to fight for, but can anybody really say the English language is disappearing? Just watch TV or surf the Web!"

"It doesn't mean much to me, either," Tibor said, slipping his thumbs through his belt loops as he lounged to a halt.

"You sound like you don't really agree with me." Jane met his eyes with a directness that demolished his advantage in height.

"A few months ago maybe I wouldn't have. But I've been having an identity crisis."

"That sounds interesting." Taking a half-step towards him, Jane said: "Didn't you have a beard when I saw you on Sherbrooke Street?"

"That was part of it. I grew a beard, then I shaved it off. I moved from the West Island to the Plateau." He shook his head. "I still can't think of that neighbourhood as the Plateau. That's its yuppie name. When I was growing up there it was the East End, the French Part — the place that poor people like us lived."

Jane smiled with an oddly forgiving look. "Where are you parked, Mr. Identity Crisis? Are we going the same way?"

"I'm parked at the bus stop. I sold the Honda to pay Sue's fucking lawyer." He felt embarrassed at having uttered the swear-word — not because it was the first time Jane had heard him use this sort of language, but because the word seemed obscenely revealing of the lust that entered him as he stared at her in that dress.

"Does that mean I can give you a lift home?"

As though sensing his sudden paralysed disorientation, she cuffed him on the sleeve. He took a step forward and followed her to her car. The heat of sensuality had given way to a low-grade tension and a complicity that felt deeper than it could possibly be. Leaning back in the passenger seat of Jane's Renault, he released a long, flat breath.

Jane swung onto the steep incline of Chemin de la Côte-des-Neiges. As they climbed the hillside, the tilt of the car pushed them back in their seats like astronauts. They crawled past the Montreal General Hospital and the dark Viennese-looking towers of the Gleneagles apartment block rising against the sky on the crest of the hill above Marianopolis College, where he had studied for two years in his teens. That had been his first contact with rich kids, though it hadn't prepared him for meeting Sue.

Sparse rain struck the windshield and spread into glimmering sickles.

"What's the story with you and Sue?" Jane asked, turning on the wipers.

"We split up a year ago. We were fighting over the stuff until last month, when I caved in and let her rip me off. It would have bankrupted me to keep fighting. Her daddy buys all the best lawyers."

"You're lucky there weren't any children."

"Yeah." Unnerved by her quick, unfathomable glance, he stared out the window. "Tomorrow morning I'm taking the train to Toronto to sign the settlement at her lawyer's office."

"Are you going to see her?"

He shook his head. "I tried to call her last week to bury the hatchet but I got her machine. Would you believe it? Her message is bilingual! *Je ne peux pas répondre à votre appel en ce moment mais si vous laissez un message après le signal qui suit je vous rappellerai dès que possible* . . . In ten years I didn't hear her speak that much French."

"They take the one-way ticket down the 401 because they hate Quebec and when they get to Toronto suddenly they become bilingual."

"It's easy to be bilingual in Toronto."

"Me, I don't like Toronto." Jane made the sharp right turn onto Camillien-Houde. They went down, then up again into a volcanic rockscape where for a second it was difficult to believe that they were anywhere near a city. As they climbed along the back of the Mountain, the Notre-Dame-des-Neiges cemetery spread away on the left in a battlefield sweep of tomb-studded meadows. "What are you doing now?"

"I quit my job. That was part of my identity crisis. My artsy buddy Jean-Yves was going to hire me as business manager on this movie he wanted to make, but he didn't get the subvention. So I'm on a six-month contract with an insurance company. It could turn into a job, but I don't think I want it. I'm looking for something else. It's not easy — you don't make many friends when you're an internal auditor."

"What about your friends at the Anglo rights group?"

"Yeah, right," he said, fending off her smile. She kept grinning. He reached over and rubbed her thigh with the palm of his hand. The movement, a kind of joshing retort for her teasing, took him by surprise. He was shocked by his own unthinking audacity. It carried him back to being a big gangly sixteen-year-old who could crush opposition forwards against the boards but didn't understand his own strength or anything else about his body. One night in the minivan home after a game against a team from the West Island, he had started stroking one of the cheerleaders, a girl he had never noticed before. He didn't have a clue whether he even liked this girl. Later that night he and the girl lost their virginity together on the sofa in her parents' finished basement. A dash of that same breakneck lack of control was storming through him. He hadn't intended to make a pass at Jane — his gesture had not been meant that way. Wasn't she living with someone?

Colour swamped her cheeks. "You don't hit on a woman while she's at the wheel."

"I didn't mean — "

"Sure you didn't mean it."

Unable to gauge the extent of her anger, he changed the subject. They were descending through the steep cutting in the rock to the lip of the Mountain, where the city's East End stretched below them to the rim of the early dusk in tens of thousands of low-rise blocks of brick and stone. A light pressure squeezing his ears from the descent, Tibor said: "When I was at McGill I used to give tours to rich kids who thought the city was just McGill and Westmount. I'd bring them up here and tell them, '*That*'s Montreal, you jerks! Everything out there — that's where most people live!'"

"That whole student life is so foreign to me," Jane said, staring into the oncoming dusk as they curved down out of the trees towards Avenue du Parc. "Silly me, I got married at eighteen, so when I went to university at Concordia I was a divorced working woman of twenty-five. It was night school, I went part-time. There was none of that campus stuff." Stopping at the traffic light, she looked across at him. Overhead a streetlight came on, the glare throwing the near side of Jane's face into shadow. Her gaze sought him out as it had on the street when she had challenged his views on English signs; this time her expression was less daunting. Was she still angry with him for pawing her? How should he interpret her pursed lips and narrowed eyes? "I was getting divorced around the time we were working together. Do you remember that?"

"I remember you being kind of subdued."

"Yeah, I guess that must have been how I was at work. Subdued."

The word cancelled out the possibility of further conversation. The traffic closed in and the sidewalks were thronged with people. The Plateau was waking up for the evening. Through a lighted window Tibor glimpsed three portly men in dress shirts gathered around a pool table in a barren corner store. The bars whose decor rotated every few months were filling up with students and punks and greying bohemians; the wrought-iron railings of the walk-up duplexes and triplexes on the sidestreets sank into the dark as the Renault edged forward.

"It must be great living here."

"Yeah, it's a great neighbourhood." It was the required reply. Every time he uttered it, Tibor felt he was confessing to countless pick-ups and trysts. In fact, for all the evenings he had whiled away in bars and cafés on Boulevard St-Laurent and Rue St-Denis, he had not had sex during the year since he and Sue had separated. Now and then an eddy of memory would catch him, tugging him back to the insatiability that had possessed them when they had first got together, the sheer *bodiness* of his being during those early months with Sue when he seemed always to be naked and squeezing and licking and caressing. He sometimes glimpsed that intensely physical alertness in the faces of elated young couples careering down the streets of the Plateau. It felt incomprehensible to him, as other formerly familiar sensations had become incomprehensible.

Jane parked the Renault beneath the mournful glow of a Parisian-style black streetlamp.

"You didn't have to park," Tibor said, "I could have just hopped out — "

She slid out of the car, came around to his side, opened his door and gestured to him to stand up. When he climbed out of the passenger seat, she swung the door shut and locked her arm through his. The weight of her body, bearing in against his side, made him catch his breath. They paced towards his ugly low rise building, each step simultaneously a savouring and a mounting of tension. Jane's smile grew wider. Tibor stared at her face, her waist. He looked at his feet.

They walked in the front door, up the two short flights of stairs and in the door of his two-and-a-half-room apartment in the assembly-line 1960s-built low-rise. Jane said: "I used to live in apartments like this after I got di — "

Tibor kissed her absurdly wide mouth, his hands running over her back to wring out all of Jane's warmth and concentrate it in the heated tussling of their mouths. They kissed until they ran out of breath. Arm-in-arm, they promenaded across his tiny bedroom to draw the curtain.

"Unzip me," Jane said, putting down her handbag and offering him the back of her dress. He reached around her and cupped her fuchsia breasts with his palms, rocking his hands as he drew her against him to nuzzle her neck. "Just unzip it," she whispered. A moment later she was folding her dress over the back of the chair by his window. Dimly aware of the grumble of traffic and voices from the crowded streets, he stared at the underwater wash of light that filtered through his filmy green-patterned curtain and rode the curves of Jane's flesh from her hip to her shoulder. His breathing tightened; he scrambled out of his clothes. In bed, the first smack of the milky scent of her body revived a thousand dormant fibres in his flesh. He was waking up sexually, just as he had at sixteen: unused nerve-ends that had gone to sleep in the last year tortured him as they jangled into wakefulness. He delved with his tongue after a glint of light hair nestled amid the dark sprigs in Jane's armpit. He kneaded and bit and inhaled her as, giggling, she tickled his thighs and teased his penis. He twisted, descended, nibbled her thighs, then licked and probed between them with a lazy, lingering absorption that lifted him out of time. Later, he heard Jane's murmuring rise to a moan, felt her body heave; felt himself, still unsated, heaving with her.

She kissed him on the mouth. "Your turn."

He reached towards the low chest of drawers next to the bed with a gesture he hoped looked practised. The dozen condoms he had scattered in the top drawer when he moved in were gathering dust.

Jane caught his wrist. "No."

"No?" He tried to make out her expression in the gloom.

"It's not necessary and I don't want it."

Meaning she was on the pill? Meaning she trusted him not to have done anything stupid recently? They clutched each other rib to rib as he fitted himself inside her. His mind was dizzy, yet, at first, he felt desolated. His initial gliding half-thrust brought him the news that he had lost the thrifty dance he and Sue had perfected over ten years of marriage. Jane's proportions were wrong, her breasts too large, her body slumberous by comparison with Sue's whippet-like carriage, hardened in recent years by her growing aquafit addiction. He had to learn how to make love again. He was the big gawky kid who took out wingers breaking in along the boards with body-checks whose technique he didn't understand. He toiled to match his movements to Jane's pulse. He was a body pursuing bodiness — until his own shocking groan closed off the chase.

He gasped as they slipped apart.

Later Jane, returning from the bathroom, tossed a towel at him. She rolled into bed and nuzzled his shoulder. "All right, I'm glad you came to that meeting."

"The parties you don't want to go to are the ones that change your life." Sue had told him that each time she had inveigled him into accompanying her to a stultifying Westmount wine-tasting or a steak-searing barbecue at some mogul's spread in the Laurentians. Her claim had always puzzled him: he and Sue had met in a yawningly ordinary way, as undergraduates at McGill who were taking the same courses. He explained this to Jane, feeling the post-coital languor in her limbs tighten, and not caring because suddenly he was angry that he was single and she wasn't; angry that the implication that this encounter might change their lives should make her tense; angry that their lovemaking might not mean as much to her as — evidently, unwillingly, pitifully — it did to him. "She used to call meetings like that 'the duty calls.' 'The duty calls are the ones that change your life.' That was what she always said — and that was how she met that oily bastard — "

"How did she meet him?"

"At some goddamn shareholders' thing for a company her daddy gave her stocks in. They held one of their dinners at the Quatre Saisons and the jerk flew up from Toronto for it."

"That was how I met Walid. At a boring business lunch." He sensed her eyes concentrating on him. He stared at the ceiling. It was about time she brought up Walid. He lay still and waited until, with a short sigh and an arm looped around his shoulder, Jane said: "He's a very traditional man. Sometimes I feel like a Muslim wife . . . But ever since I got divorced I've had this crazy pattern. As soon as I settle down with one guy I have to have another one."

"Have you talked to a shrink about this?"

"I don't want to talk to a shrink. It makes my life more exciting!" When he failed to budge, she said: "Don't pretend to be shocked. Half the Plateau lives that way."

"That's what everybody in the suburbs thinks about the Plateau." The conversation was making him feel uptight— *pas un vrai Montréalais*, as Jean-Yves would say. Tibor wasn't sure he was equal to the image of *le vrai Montréal*; not now, at thirty-seven. He had viewed the building-blocks of middle-class life — a working marriage, a job, a car, a house in the West Island — as divine blessings. He had been stunned to find himself in possession of all these gifts, incredulous to realize that he was married to Sue, with her blonde good looks and Square Mile pedigree. Ten years had been barely long enough to accustom him to thinking of himself as Sue's husband. Now that the marriage — along with the car, the job and the house in the West Island — had vanished, he felt himself tossed into a squirming nothingness where men and women, work and leisure, English, French and Hungarian, slapped against one another in ways he felt crustily resistant to trying to understand. He just wanted everything to be simple. Why must the city become more fluid as he grew less willing to change?

He tried to explain some of this to Jane. "*Tranquille!*" she said. "Relax. Aren't you freer than before?"

"Sure," he said. How could he say freedom wasn't a good thing? His parents would leap up from their graves to denounce him. "But I want to know what this means, too," he said, squeezing her around the ribs. "What happens to these extra guys you get involved with — the ones you're not living with?"

"Sometimes I move in with them."

In spite of himself, he felt hope slash through him. "But then you end up leaving them for the next guy, right?"

"I think this will end. I can feel it's not going to go on much longer. Something's going to happen to end it — it's just the way I am now, the way I've been for the last few years." Nudging his head around, she kissed him on the mouth. "Tibor, I was really happy when I saw you standing there with all those old fossils."

"The competition wasn't too tough."

"I *mean* it." She laid her cheek on his chest. "It's so weird how we end up places. How you end up in bed with people you never would have met if things had been different. Walid wouldn't even be in Quebec if his family's house in Beirut hadn't been bombed."

"I wouldn't be here if my uncle hadn't been killed."

"An uncle in Hungary?"

"Yeah. I never met him. He must have been really young. In 1956 the Russians sent the tanks in and the Hungarians fought like hell. Not like those wimpy Czechs in Prague in 1968 who went out to talk to the tank drivers and ask them to please go home. We went out there and murdered the fuckers. They strung up KGB guys from the lampposts. When the tanks came into Budapest the young Hungarian guys got grenades and rolled them between the tracks. My uncle Arpád died that way. We don't know how. His friends said he blew up a tank and the Russians shot him, but it's possible he pulled the pin out too quickly and blew himself up, and the friends just said that."

"Wait a minute. You weren't born then?"

"No, they'd been in Montreal for seven years when I was born. I say 'us' because it's my family. I feel like it happened to me. Arpád was my dad's brother. I should have gotten to know him and I never did." The room was growing cooler. He hauled the covers over their bodies. "He died because he knew what his duty was. Somebody invades your country, you fight them. You don't think about the fact that maybe you're going to get killed."

Jane looked at the wall, as though considering what to say next.

"But it crushed my parents. My dad, especially. He never got over it. After that he didn't want to stay in Hungary. It was too painful. A couple of weeks later they sneaked across the border.

They hitchhiked to Vienna and went straight to the Canadian embassy. That's how we ended up here."

"And that's how we ended up here," Jane said, sending her hand scurrying down the front of his body tweaking all the way. When he turned to enclose her in his arms, she pressed a finger to his lips. "Tibor, I'm really, really sorry about this but I'm going to have to go. I told Walid I wouldn't be back for supper, but this is getting ridiculous. It's almost ten o'clock."

"I have a train to catch tomorrow morning." He let his head subside onto the pillow.

She kissed him and got up. He turned on the bedside light and sat with the soles of his feet pressed flat against the tile floor, watching her dress. She responded to his attention with a flushed smile. Had he ever seen a woman lighted up from within like that?

As he zipped up the back of her dress, repressing his yearning to ask when they would see each other again, Jane took a harried glance at her watch. "Shit! Tibor, I know this is weird, but I really have to call him now." She reached for her handbag, shook loose her cell-phone and punched it with her thumb. Couldn't she wait until she was in the Renault? He watched her clapping the phone to her ear and speaking past it into the blank wall where he had been meaning to put up a poster. Her voice slipped into a high, fluting French that sounded less Québécois than the French he had heard her speak at the office. *"Je suis désolée, Walid. J'ai rencontré un ancien ami. On est allés prendre un verre et parler des bons vieux temps. J'ai pas de tout remarqué l'heure . . . Mais j'arrive, là, j'arrive . . . "* She lowered the mobile and faced him with a shifting smile. "I told him the truth. I just left out the details."

"And you added some. We didn't actually have a drink together."

"Okay," she said, after a moment's hesitation. "Why don't we do that next week? How about Tuesday at six at Bistro Quatre? Walid's going to Paris for three days to see his suppliers." Her eyes narrowed. "Maybe we can spend the whole night together."

He flung his arms around her. As his palms soaked up the warmth of her back, he thought that next time it would be Walid who unzipped her dress; in two hours' time Jane would be in bed with Walid, possibly making love with him. He tried to stifle his jealousy. He was living in the Plateau! Could he succumb to middle-class anxiety simply because the woman with whom he had just made love had another lover? "It's fantastic we ran into each other," he said as he followed her to the door. "Don't disappear!"

"I'm not going anywhere," Jane said. He held her a moment too long and felt her impatient stiffening. She turned and hurried down the stairs. In a second he was back in the small apartment, listening to the hacking of the traffic. Aside from his rumpled bed, the towel on the floor and the sense of hollow satiation seeping through his limbs, no sign existed that Jane had entered his life.

He straightened the bedcovers, went out to the *dépanneur* for a bottle of cheap red wine and sat up half the night flipping around on the radio in search of stations that played good jazz. His alarm clock slugged him out of his sleep with grit behind his eyes. Punch-drunk, he struggled onto the Métro, then stumbled through the bowels of Place Bonaventure to the train station. The long trip to Toronto began with a slinking loop through ancient redbrick slums. He dozed off in defiance of the bright, clear dawn, dwelling on how Hungarian Boulevard St-Laurent used to be: until recently you only had to board the 55 bus to hear Magyar spoken. A dry-goods store near the junction with Prince-Arthur, staffed by old men who knew about Uncle Arpád and had come to his father's funeral in stiff suits and dented black hats, had kept going until the late 1990s. Whenever he wandered in there, the old men would speak to him in Magyar and try to sell him one of the heavy, red-patterned carpets that he thought of as Hungarian, even though Sue, to his discomfort, called them "Turkish." Nearby, on the opposite side of St-Laurent, a gift shop had specialized in Zsolnay porcelain, green-and-white Hungarian Catholic calendars with St. Stephen's Day circled in red, dolls in fine lace dresses, folk-music cassettes packaged in photocopied-looking covers. He had gone into the shop as a child with his father and Ildikó in the lull after a pre-Christmas blizzard that had cleared St-Laurent of people, smothering the street in snowdrifted silence. They had bought his mother a Christmas present of a dish towel featuring a sprawling map of Greater Hungary — the country in its full expansive glory, not its present dismembered form. Tibor's mother had been so moved by the gift that she had pinned it to the wall over the supper table. Tibor had studied the map every night while he ate. Geography classes had made him aware that the point his family referred to as the Hungarian city of Pozsony appeared in his school atlas as Bratislava, Czechoslovakia, while the blip he had learned to recognize as Nándorfehérvár, in southern Hungary, was identified by the atlas as Belgrade, Yugoslavia. Accustomed to bi- and trilingualism, he worried little about the discrepancies, shrugging off the historical blindness of

Canadian school teachers. When, in high school, the election of the Parti Québécois altered some street-names and imposed French signs on the fronts of the stores along St-Laurent, Tibor was left cold by the fury of his classmates who had surnames like Davis and MacPherson. Why did these changes surprise them? His parents would do the same, if Hungary were to regain its lost territory: duty would demand the enforcement of Hungarian signs in bilingual Transylvania, Vojvodina and Slovakia. Marrying Sue had changed his mind on this question. He had adopted the freedom-of-speech position and joined an Anglo rights group. But years of work in mainly French-language offices, a few months' residence in the Plateau and now the warmth of Jane's mouth had flipped his views back again, persuading him that, as the only French place in North America, Quebec had the right to require French signs . . . Why couldn't he simply *know* what was right, as his parents had done? He slipped into a herky-jerky dream where Uncle Arpád, bright-faced and slender as in the one surviving photograph, tumbled on his side on the dark street walled in by Habsburg-era apartment blocks. Arpád reached towards the grinding rumble of the tank to roll the grenade between its tracks. The tank veered and drove over his shoulder, and before he could scream the grenade went off, obliterating the part of him that had been under the tank and leaving the rest of his body convulsing on the stones in a final severed cluster of blood-smeared life.

Was that how it had been? Had Arpád died slowly? Is he still dying, Tibor wondered, in my goddamn wishy-washiness? (Did his sister Ildikó in Vancouver, the mother of two teenage sons who could not locate Hungary on the map, worry about these things?) He felt terminally hungover. The generation of

1956 was dying. He rubbed his eyes and ordered a coffee and a danish from a man passing with a trolley. Maybe he would feel better once he had signed the settlement. He rehearsed all the arguments he could have with Sue if she were in the room. The argument where he accused her of despising his immigrant upbringing and she replied that he had married her for her money. The argument where she asked him if he was ever going to get promoted and he asked her if anybody in her family had ever worked his way up, or had they always bought the company? The argument —

He fell asleep again and woke as the train entered Union Station. His stomach queasy, he found a taxi and rode to the Best Western on Bloor Street. He had just enough time before his appointment with Sue's lawyers to lie down for half an hour, shower, then dress in his blue suit. When he reached the office he was ushered into a room where two lawyers, a man and a woman, shook his hand and called him "sir" in tones that made it sound like an insult. Pleased to note that they were both much shorter than he, Tibor spun out his advantage by remaining standing as he scanned the agreement. His disappointment at Sue's absence was keener than he had expected. The male lawyer, speaking in a Toronto lockjaw accent that sounded like a foreign language, outlined the terms of the agreement. Tibor listened in enervated absent-mindedness. Sue's father, in his fervour to ensure that no East End immigrant would get his grimy fingers on a cent of his daughter's inheritance, had confiscated most of the money Tibor had contributed over the years to the family's second cottage in the Townships and the time-share in the Dominican Republic; all Tibor had been able to salvage was a nearly-fair assessment of the payments he had made on the house in the West Island. All too familiar with the agreement's details, he interrupted the lawyer, initialled two clauses and signed at the bottom of the last page. He signed and initialled a second copy. Five minutes later he was out on the street and his marriage was truly, finally, terrifyingly, over. Lacking children to shunt back and forth, he and Sue need never speak to each other again.

He walked west on Bloor to the stretch that used to be lined with Hungarian shops and restaurants. At least two of the restaurants had closed since his last trip to Toronto. As in Montreal, the old refugees were dying; Arabic script and bursts of Spanish poked out where polysyllabic Magyar had prevailed. Tibor entered a nearly empty restaurant and sat down at a plain brown table. He hesitated at the sight of the tall young waitress's high cheekbones, finally ordering in English while reading out the names of the dishes from the bilingual menu in Magyar. The waitress took his order, scrutinized him, then said: "*Köszönöm szépen.*" A moment later a shambling man in his sixties emerged from the back of the restaurant. "*Honnan jön?*" he asked. "Where are you from?"

"Montreal."

"Montreal! I thought you were from Europe. My daughter told me there was this guy from Hungary in the restaurant."

They tried out the names of acquaintances on each other, but they knew none of the same people. Speaking Magyar made Tibor feel as if he were skating: it was all going too fast and he was never sure when he had put a foot wrong. When the daughter arrived with Tibor's *bakonyi betyárleves* — outlaw soup, the perfect meal for a man who had just become officially single — the proprietor wished him a good supper and vanished.

By nine o'clock Tibor was depressed; by ten, after a lingering drink at the bar of a hotel farther along Bloor, he was dying to see Jane again. He thought of former Montrealers now living in Toronto whom he could call and one by one eliminated them from consideration. He trailed back to the hotel, set his alarm clock and, barely able to face a second five-hour train trip, drank his way up Lake Ontario and the St. Lawrence River. He kept drinking when he reached Montreal. He staggered home at three-thirty in the morning, his blue suit crushed. It took him most of the weekend to recover. He shuffled around the apartment trying to screen out the sound of the traffic as he played the cassettes he and Sue had danced to as students, and waited for Jane to call. He realized he didn't know her phone number. None of the Mertons listed in the phone book was she, and who knew what Walid's last name might be? And then there was her cellular. How did you find the number for a cellphone? He wondered whether Jane remembered his last name, Hajnóczy, or would know how to spell it. In the end all that mattered was that they were going to spend the night together. Their needs had become complementary. For once, his timing might be right. Thank God for the duty calls! One day he would write to Sue to thank her for her advice.

All day Monday and Tuesday at work he felt his reawakened nerve ends twitching. He worked like a man in hibernation, his energy stored up in the aggravating weight of his sluggish semi-permanent erection. His distraction didn't matter: insurance companies didn't want their employees to think. His job as an internal auditor had demanded perpetual vigilance, constant questioning, sufficient self-awareness to vet his own methods of analysis and understand what his approach to a problem might have caused him to miss. It had twisted him into an acuteness of perception that he had felt dwindling in recent months. Sue had claimed that his job had turned him into an anti-social loner. She had grown up among hearty, back-slapping men who got themselves appointed to the board . . . What kind of men had Jane grown up around? He had a notion that her background was middle-class, suburban, vaguely cultured and unstable. Hadn't her father produced documentary films? Weren't her parents divorced? His memories of their conversations during the distant days when they had worked together were blotted out by his more recent memories of her body.

After work on Tuesday he went home and exchanged his grey suit, white shirt and red tie for beige slacks, a light brown dress shirt and a dark brown corduroy jacket. The late afternoon had turned cool, dusk gathered beneath the trees; another epic Montreal winter was on the way. He approached Bistro Quatre up the red-cobbled incline of Avenue Duluth. The men sitting on the street corners were speaking Portuguese, the kids tearing past them yelled at each other in English that turned to French in mid-sentence. The black plunge of the Mountain closed off the end of the street, causing the evening light to waver on the redbrick walls and the crusts of decaying wooden gingerbread. For Tibor, the pleasures of the Plateau came mingled with fear. He worried that he would spend the rest of his life ambling around these easygoing, picturesque streets, bouncing off people, and not knowing where he belonged.

Reaching the corner of Boulevard St-Laurent, he felt his breath contract as he glimpsed the back of Jane's head through the glass. The shimmer of her thick hair pulled him across the street. He went down the steps into the bistro. The small, circular brass tables he remembered had been replaced by tables that were larger and squarer. Jane smiled, offering him her cheek as he leaned over her. Nudging her head around with his palm, he kissed her on the lips. She blushed. Tibor sat down, irritated by the surge of his erection and the squareness of the tables, which placed him across from Jane. Over his shoulder he heard a group of francophone artists arranging a vernissage. The bistro's setting, just below street-level, sent pedestrians streaming past at the height of his shoulders. "How are you?" he asked. Once he had ordered his coffee he looked at her again, perched on her chair with her hands stowed below the table. Dressed in a pale blue skirt-and-jacket combination, she appeared to have come straight from work.

"Oh, Tibor."

It was a relief to hear her voice. "What's wrong?" he said, seeing her smile grow more fixed. "Did you have a bad day?"

She sipped her coffee. "I'm all right. How was your trip to Toronto?"

He felt thwarted, outraged, unwilling to speak until she became the warm, sexual woman with whom he had fled the Anglo rights meeting. Her mouth looked less wide than he remembered, her cheeks more rotund. He told her about his trip, not meaning to wallow in his misery yet conscious of how hellish it sounded. "I missed you," he concluded. "When I got back I wanted so badly to call you, but I couldn't find your goddamn number."

The light picked out wrinkles in the corners of Jane's eyes. She held her hands clasped below the table. Outside the street was growing gloomy. "I went to the doctor yesterday," she murmured.

"What . . . ?" His memory of her fingers detaining his wrist intensified his frustration at being unable to see her hands. "Are you . . . ?"

"Yes." She stared at him. "Yes, Tibor."

"God, why didn't we use a condom?"

Jane laughed. Her hand swatted his shoulder. "Dipstick! Don't you know the facts of life? It's Walid's baby. I wouldn't know yet if it was yours!"

"You're *pregnant.*"

"Of course." Her voice grew low and purposeful. "You can see what this means, Tibor. I'm thirty-five. It's time to stop acting like a party girl. This is the sign I've been waiting for . . . Walid's a good man, there are levels where we don't connect but most marriages are coincidences . . . who you end up with. The main thing is whether you want to make it work, and I think we both want to raise a family."

She had spoken so swiftly, with a determination he did not recognize, that the replies he could think of felt pointless. They all depended on him: his feelings, his loneliness, his loss of direction. Jane had only to invoke the child she was carrying to shrink these things to triviality. He peered out at the young couples loping downhill along the head-high sidewalk.

"So the baby was there . . . the other night?" The thought that a third ghostly presence — Walid and Jane's child — had attended their lovemaking made him seize the edge of the table. He envisaged his unsheathed penis grazing a miniature Walid: he imagined him plump, smiling, bald. He was a klutz and an idiot. Or had Jane deceived him? No, that wasn't fair; he had known what he wanted from the moment he spotted her at the meeting. What he had failed to realize was that sex was only the beginning of what he wanted from her.

"Are you all right?" Jane lifted her hands and spread them flat on the table. She squared her shoulders. "I feel like a completely different person than I did last week."

Tibor struggled to speak, then drew a breath and opted for silence. He stared at Jane's wide firm face, wishing he could absorb her knowledge, certain that, whatever he had been seeking, Jane had found it.

BEYOND BLISS

"VIVIAN," RAY SAID. "We've got something to tell you."

He smiled, and Vivian knew with confident certainty that
the perfect moment had arrived. Acceptance. Ray and Debbie
were her first Canadian friends, fruit of her realization that
she could not spend the rest of her life as the petite English girl
who had followed her rich Canadian boyfriend to Toronto. One
could not live forever on bliss, as wise Uncle Cecil said. Uncle
Cecil had predicted her swift return to Hampstead. Yet when
her euphoria at Dave's touch lapsed into comfortable habit, she
felt no inclination to return to England. Dave *liked* her, really
liked her womanliness with a wide-grinned, big-handed, open-
mouthed pleasure. She would never leave him for an English
boy who had been sent to a posh school to take his canings like
a man and regard girls as horrid. The boys she had known in
London would be at Oxford, or perhaps at Cambridge or LSE;
she could not think of one who was worth the move back to
Britain. Had she remained in England she would have been
at Oxford herself by now — likely at Somerville or St. Hilda's,

or at one of the men's colleges that was starting to accept women — though on the whole Oxford was less important for a girl. What mattered was getting on in life. Yet getting on worked differently in Canada.

"This is going to be great," Debbie said, rolling up the sleeve of her batik shirt as she stubbed out her cigarette. Posters of Ho Chi Minh and Jimi Hendrix hung on the wall, but it was the lugubrious voice of Leonard Cohen that maundered from the café's transistor radio.

"We're going to be famous." Ray's smile folded in on itself in the aggressively complacent expression that Torontonians adopted when asserting their importance in the face of Canadian insignificance. Vivian could see perspiration gleaming below the fraying blond spar that reached farther forward than the rest of Ray's hair. A pleat appeared in his scarlet cravat as he leaned over to meet Debbie's eyes with one of those looks that made Vivian wonder whether they were not lovers after all. Had Debbie not regaled her with accounts of her bedroom antics with a bearded American draft dodger, she would have assumed Debbie and Ray were a couple. "We've got a lease on the Wheelman Gallery and a grant from the Canada Council. We're going to start publishing books next spring. Look out! Here comes Wheelman Press!"

"We wanted you to be the first to know," Debbie said, pinching Vivian's sleeve. "You're our most literary friend."

"Whose work do you intend to publish?"

Ray and Debbie grew still. Forthright, factual inquiries, which came naturally in London, got her in trouble here.

Ray mentioned the names of people he had studied with at the University of Toronto who had gone on to publish poems and stories. Vivian grew conscious of his accent, which a few months earlier she would have been unable to distinguish from an American accent, and whose most noticeable peculiarity was not the "ou" sound, as Canadians imagined, but an oddly fluid "r." Her awareness of the tones of Ray's voice made her feel abstracted from the conversation, caught on the outside of Ray and Debbie's bubble of complicity. Wheelman Press. She had guessed this was coming. It would be a wonderful first step in her Canadian career.

"That sounds splendid," she said, when Ray's voice petered out. "I must say I'm delighted. Who will be working at Wheelman Press?"

"Just us," Debbie said. Releasing Vivian's wrist, she reached across the table to touch Ray's arm. "It's our baby, right, Ray?"

"Our beautiful baby. With the people we know, the books we're gonna be able to get, we'll be famous."

Vivian was surprised by the effort required to conceal her disappointment: she felt horribly betrayed. If she was their most literary friend, why weren't they inviting her to join them? Foreignness, she supposed. It was terribly difficult to realize that here one was a foreigner. She knew she must say something: the right thing; any response that betrayed bitterness would do her in. She thought of others who suffered the exclusion of being foreigners. Suddenly she knew what to say. "You should publish Erich Mueller."

"Erich Mueller!" Debbie said. "He's a fascist! He *supports* the war in Vietnam!"

"One needn't agree with his politics in order to publish him. It would give Wheelman Press enormous visibility. Mueller has a large international reputation, particularly in Europe, but it's based almost entirely on the publicity surrounding his escape from East Germany. Little of his work has been translated. If you play your cards right Wheelman Press could become Mueller's avenue to the English-speaking world."

"I'm not going near that creep," Debbie said.

Ray was silent. On the radio Leonard Cohen had yielded to Ian and Sylvia. Dave had taken her to see Ian and Sylvia perform in Yorkville during her second weekend in Toronto; it had been her introduction to being polite about Canadian culture.

Ray continued to look at her, his small blue eyes contracting to beady shrewdness. Vivian imagined she saw a reflection of Uncle Cecil in those eyes: cold, clever Uncle Cecil, who nourished a rumour that he had slept with Katherine Mansfield and at least one of her male lovers, had manoeuvred himself to the top of the London publishing industry while continuing to scribble on the side. Uncle Cecil would lend her a magisterial trans-Atlantic hand. If she offered him Canadian publication for his book on the customs of the Marsh Arabs, he would almost certainly send her British and European novelists. But first she must have a base.

The silence went on. Seeing Ray wavering she decided to risk making one of those haughty English statements that sometimes offended Canadians, but, in the proper circumstances, brought them to heel. "Erich Mueller," she said, "was the only person in Toronto I had heard of before I moved here."

"If you think I'm going to touch a page he's written," Debbie said, "you can forget it."

Ray stared at the checkered table cloth. "The manuscripts are in German, I guess. We could find a translator. There's a guy

I knew at Victoria College . . . The problem is, Mueller's never going to talk to me because I wrote a letter to the editor after he published that article in *The Globe* attacking Chairman Mao."

"Don't expect me to talk to him," Debbie said. "Anyway, doesn't this go against everything we said we stood for? Wheelman Press is supposed to be a *radical* voice. We're supposed to publish *Canadian* writers."

"You're right," Ray said. His tiny eyes met Vivian's eyes for a glancing, wistful instant. "It's a shame, but Erich Mueller isn't really what Wheelman Press is about."

~

"Some Kraut called for you," Dave said. His teasing, so much more easygoing than snippy British irony, always made Vivian laugh. "*Ees Veeveeian there? Ve haf vays of making her come to ze phone!*"

"Oh, you are a pill," she said, kissing him. The late afternoon sunlight entered their flat in a pattern cut by the hump-backed branch of the elm outside the window. Of course the place where they lived was not a flat but an apartment. And it was enormous: four times the size of any digs she could have afforded in London. That, she had explained to Uncle Cecil in her last letter, was why one emigrated. "That's Erich Mueller. He's frightfully famous in Europe but no one here seems to grasp his importance."

"Except Vivian, eh?" he said, looking up from his quadra-phonic sound system. He had been working for days on the perfect speaker arrangement. Wires ran in all directions from the record player beneath the window. His Neil Young and Buffalo Springfield records still did not sound right, the bass continuing to strum alone in the corner of the room. He looped a wire around the back of a hassock and pushed the couch against the wall. "Is this a business opportunity, honey?"

"It might be," she said, laying her hands on his hips as he stood up. "Do you mind?"

"How could I? You're amazing, Vivian. I'm telling you, you could do anything."

She kissed him again. One of Dave's peculiarities, which he shared with other Canadians she had met, was that statements which sounded fraudulent were often sincere. If an English bloke had spoken like that she would have assumed he was mocking her. She had to translate to understand that her plans had received an endorsement.

Neither of them had learned to cook when young — Vivian's family had servants and Dave had a mother — so most nights they ate out. Vivian considered this one of the more miserable aspects of Toronto existence. There were so few decent places to eat, so little variety beyond the regulation pizza restaurants and a few souvlaki houses which lay far out on Danforth Avenue and were too grim to set foot in. In desperation, she had learned to share Dave's fondness for steak and potatoes. As they ate in a Bloor Street steakhouse, Dave alluded to his work. He maintained a comforting vagueness about the details of board meetings and new investments. Her own father, who had been "something in the City," had never spoken of his work in London's financial district. Men, she felt, ought not to talk about their work, and women ought not to ask. She appreciated Dave's equally supportive lack of curiosity towards her attempt to establish a career. "I think we know just enough about one another," she said, looping her arm around his high waist as they left the restaurant, "to find each other tantalizingly mysterious."

In the morning, drowsy with lovemaking, she watched Dave shrug himself into his open-necked white shirt, black slacks and black suit-jacket. He had stopped wearing a tie every day and his thick, straight black hair was inching over the tops of his ears. His right eyebrow was developing an eccentric bulge. As he patted on his aftershave lotion, Vivian felt enchanted to be with him.

Spending her life in Toronto was a less galvanizing prospect than spending her life with Dave. Yet her two commitments were inseparable: beyond bliss lay compromise. The thought came home to her later that morning when, after a quick phone call to Erich Mueller, she walked south, then boarded the College streetcar going west. The city's long flat north-south streets looked as desolate as unmarked trails; the merest English footpath had more history. She craved the density of sensation of a London street: the people packed together in the rain, the crowds struggling out of the underground stations, small hidden doors, flyways and alleys spinning off at erratic angles, the newspaper vendors with the headlines scrawled on white sheets on the fronts of their stalls, the elaborate close-set façades of blocks of Georgian flats, the voices of hawkers and yobbos and toffs colliding over the shrieking brakes of the big black taxis. Funny that she had taken it all for granted. How the bustle of London would thrill her now! The floor of the streetcar shuddered beneath her feet. Here one had to be observant to discern activity. Cultural life was similar: the merest lifting of the dust was cause for wonder. It would do these people good, she felt, thinking of the city in general at the same time that she thought of Ray and Debbie, to confront certifiable cultural achievement. Even if that achievement took the form of Erich Mueller.

Mueller lived in a flat carved out of the top floor of a tall Victorian house one block north of College. He met her at the door wearing a polo neck shirt and grey slacks. His shoulders were hunched, his domed forehead high, his balding skull slightly pointy. His brown eyes and fringe of dark hair belied her childhood stereotype of what a German should look like. His corpulence retained a ghost of youthful robustness. "Come in, my dear. It is very good of you to visit a man the world wants to forget."

After three years in Toronto Mueller's English remained more cumbersome than that of young West Germans she knew. His foreignness struck her like a gust of hot wind, both soothing and unsettling. "I haven't forgotten you," she said. "I read *Shadowy Guest* when it came out in Britain. I thought it was a splendid book."

He guided her to a couch near the living room window. The midday sunlight drained down through the leaves outside like bright water pouring into a cistern. Mueller appeared with a drink in either hand. To her surprise, he sat down beside her. "Bad French wine," he said, handing her a glass. "That is what happens when you have the Liquor Control Board of Ontario. Here's to wine chosen by bureaucrats." He clinked her glass. "I'm glad you have liked *Shadowy Guest*. It is a minor work. And the publishers have sold the book to the wrong people — people who see the newspaper stories about me."

"You need to have more work published in English. That way you can build an audience among people who enjoy literature."

"There have been no people capable of enjoying literature since 1914. In Europe we make gestures towards a culture we have lost and here in America you understand nothing." He sipped his wine and grimaced. He edged closer to her. She felt his weight changing the shape of the couch. His utilitarian glasses made her wonder what an eye-doctor's office in East Berlin looked like. "We are corrupt and you are naive."

"Henry James," she said. "Decadent old Europe and virginal young America. Except that we are in Canada and I am British. I'm a foreigner, too. I'm still in the Commonwealth, but no one understands my irony." The perkiness of her voice took her aback.

"And no one will understand your taste. I am very happy that you want to read more of my work, but I doubt anyone else wants to. The workers prefer hockey and the ones who think they are educated prefer politics. Politics is much easier than literature, but it makes people stupid. They think they are morally superior because the Americans are fighting in Vietnam to protect them from Communism and they can do nothing but criticize." He took her hand. "Can a pretty girl like you understand that Western freedom is a poisoned gift?"

"But there must be good things about it," Vivian said, regretting her earnest tones. Allowing Mueller's warm, dry palm to continue cradling her hand, she stared at the diagonal creases running from the sides of his nose to the ends of his mouth. The flesh above the creases looked redder than the flesh below. The odour of his breath made her think of Dave's aftershave, his heaviness recalled by contrast Dave's agility on the Hampstead tennis court where she had first glimpsed him running circles around one of his English business associates. "What do you like about being here?"

"I can receive the royalties my books earn in West Germany," he said. "But publication is not the same in the West. In the East, when a magazine has published one of my poems, everyone in the country has read the poem. Everybody has thought about all of its meanings. People will whisper about my poem to their lovers. Here, even if a beautiful, intelligent girl like you publishes my book, no one will notice. They are all watching politics on television."

Vivian drew a deep breath, squeezing Mueller's hand. "I understand, Erich. But is there nothing good about Western freedom?"

"Yes," he said, "there is sex. People in the West are more open about sex." In the silence Vivian could hear the leaves outside the window rustling on their branches. Mueller looked at her from behind his steel frames. "It is impossible to imagine Western freedom without sex."

"What are you reading?" Dave said.

Vivian lay in bed, a pile of papers and a German-English dictionary on her bedside table. Her German "A"-level had stood her in better stead than she had expected. Erich's language was precise and devoid of regionalisms. She could understand nearly every scene in his bitter, lascivious novel about a writer determined to pretend that East Berlin after the construction of the Wall was Paris in the 1920s. "A novel. In German. I'm going to try to get an English translation published."

"Is it by the famous Kraut?" He pulled on his black jacket. Today he was wearing a red tie. He came over and kissed her. "You gonna stay in bed with the Kraut all day?"

"Just till I feel a little better, love. I may see Debbie in the afternoon." He knew that she had her period. Lust continued to beat through her cramped, bloated enervation, but no man could make demands of her. What a relief! Erich had exacted a high price for reading rights to his manuscript. The first time had been dreadful, in the way that Edwardian mothers warned their daughters that sex was dreadful. The second time she visited his apartment her feelings became more complicated. No experience could match her furious lovemaking with Dave, yet there was no gainsaying the change in Erich's attitude when she returned. The greedy fat boy became a courtly European gentleman. She appreciated his patience. She felt an involuntary closeness, an outsiders' entente, pinion her in the seconds prior to her orgasm — because, after that first ghastly afternoon, she had an orgasm each time they were together.

She continued to sleep with Dave at night. It was lovely. Erich's presence, though overwhelming when they were together, never intruded on her intimacy with Dave. Her afternoons in Erich's flat had snapped neatly into the space that she held apart from him. Her professional life was her own affair, as she said to Erich when he asked whether Dave knew about their encounters. Five minutes in Dave's company made her afternoons seem unreal. She told him, without feeling the slightest twinge, that she had spent the day in a meeting. "Still trying to get my foot in the door in the publishing business."

"Making any progress?" Dave said.

"Some. Though it's all rather up in the air."

To get on in life, Uncle Cecil used to say, one must be a bit of a harlot. In London harlotry was often — though by no means exclusively — confined to moral turpitude; literal-minded Canada interpreted harlotry in a more basic way. As she soaked in the tub, she mulled over the thought that an affair that intensified her feelings of foreignness was teaching her how to be a Canadian.

Debbie was sitting in the corner of the Bohemian Embassy when Vivian arrived carrying a leather satchel containing Erich's manuscript. The ashtray in front of Debbie was half full. She wore a tie-dyed T-shirt. Her wooden earrings brushed her shoulders like the ornaments of Borneo headhunters. Waving towards the small stage, she described coming here with Ray to attend a reading by a poet with tangled hair.

On the radio, Gordon Lightfoot's "Canadian Railway Trilogy" rolled along as inexorably as the city's streets. Vivian thought: she's trying to exclude me by mentioning all the people whom she knows and I don't. She felt certain that Ray had planned to include her in Wheelman Press and that it was Debbie who had insisted on keeping her out. She's afraid of me, Vivian thought, because she knows that for every person she knows in Toronto, I know three people in other countries.

Debbie's voice grew low. She was whispering about her draft dodger. Vivian said: "I always thought you and Ray — "

"Ray likes boys."

Parrying Debbie's stare, Vivian said: "You don't say? My Uncle Cecil likes boys. I'm sure they'd get along famously."

Debbie winced; today every comment between them was competitive. It would be pointless to bring up Erich's manuscript. She listened to Debbie's confidences, laughing when Debbie laughed. "I'm terribly sorry," she said, as three o'clock approached, "I must run."

They left the dark bar together. Vivian felt uncertain which way to turn. "Are you going back to the press?"

"No, I hardly ever go there. Ray and I get on each other's nerves." Debbie hesitated. "Hey, why don't you come back to my place? I've got some really smooth hash."

"That's very kind, but I'm afraid I simply must run," Vivian said. Debbie hugged her. Feeling an awkward flush rise through her face, Vivian hurried away.

When she was certain that she was out of Debbie's sight, she looked for a telephone booth. The door creaked as she closed it behind her and searched in her purse for a dime. The phone was answered on the second ring. "Wheelman Press."

"Ray, it's Vivian. There's something I simply must talk to you about."

The blond hardwood floors of the Wheelman Gallery bore scuff marks from the crated paintings that had been dragged out and the letter-head press that had been dragged in. Shelves hammered together in a hurry held boxes and files. Ray sat in an office off the gallery floor. The gallery's large windows made it light and airy; she could enjoy working here. As she entered Ray's office, Vivian noticed a second, vacant room stretching behind his. "That's Debbie's office," Ray said, responding to her scrutiny as he looked up from his battleship-grey office typewriter. "She hasn't moved in yet." Unshielded by his customary cravat, his sharp Adam's apple dipped. His folded glasses glinted in his chest pocket. "What can I do for you, Vivian?"

Grasping that he was not going to offer her a seat, she walked to the front of his desk and laid her leather satchel next to his typewriter. "Ray, in this satchel I hold the future of Wheelman Press. In this satchel I have a manuscript which, as your lead title, will attract so much attention that it will vault you into the leagues of major publishers."

He looked up with a hangdog expression, both pathetic and cunning. "You got Mueller's manuscript?" Flopped forward over his typewriter, he resembled a pudgier version of Bobby Hull, who Dave had pointed out to her on television as one of his favourite hockey players: Bobby Hull swollen up after a brutal pummelling on the rink.

"Yes, and it's brilliant. Ray, this is your chance — perhaps your only chance — to publish a major international work of fiction. This book has all of humanity in it. It has private life and it has politics, it has history and it has humour. It has sex — lots of sex." She felt herself falter. Ray gave her an odd look. She continued: "Ray, if Wheelman Press chooses Erich Mueller's *A Man Against Time* as its lead title I can promise you that my Uncle Cecil will write a blurb for the back cover. With a blurb from Uncle Cecil, you can sell the book internationally. Furthermore, if you publish a Canadian edition of Uncle Cecil's lovely book on Marsh Arabs, he will come to Toronto for the launch. I'm sure the two of you will get along splendidly, and after that he's certain to send you foreign books to publish."

When she looked down his face had broken into an imploring smile. "Well, I guess I know what you want for this. You want to be taken into the company with Debbie and me, eh?"

"No," Vivian said. "I want you to get rid of Debbie and replace her with me."

"What? Look, Vivian, I don't do stuff like that, okay? I mean Debbie's my oldest buddy. She was the first one I told I was — I mean, you just don't treat people like that." Pushing back his chair, he pointed to the room behind him. "You see that room? That's Debbie's office."

"She still hasn't moved in! Ray, you need a business partner who's here, not — " Ray bowed towards his typewriter. The bald spot on the top of his head, invisible when he was standing, winked at her like a target. "How much of the company does Debbie own?"

"Fifty per cent."

"And how much is that? How much did she put in?"

"She hasn't put in anything," he said in a suffocated voice. "I mean, she's going to pay me, she promised. But we don't have anything on paper. She has to borrow the money — "

"Tell me the amount, Ray, and I'll be here tomorrow morning with the cheque."

"Oh, shit, Vivian, I was afraid you'd do something like this." He lifted his hands and balled them into fists. "How the hell did you get Mueller to give you his manuscript?"

"State secret," she said, deflecting the lift of his chin. "Tell me the figure, Ray."

"On one condition." He was staring down at the typewriter keys. She glimpsed a sunken line running across the back of his neck. "You tell her. You tell her what we've done." His voice caught. "I couldn't face her, Vivian. After all these years . . . I really couldn't face her."

"I'll look after everything, Ray. Just remember: you're going to be famous. I'll take care of Debbie. Tomorrow I'll come back with the cheque and move into my office."

Ray shook his head. "Is nothing sacred?"

She looked at him, wondering if he was up to the job. In a soft voice she said: "Sometimes, Ray, in order to get on in life — " Then she stopped herself and simply said: "No."

The long streets looked less foreign in the evening light. Her mind focused on her chores: she must ask Dave to lend her money, arrange for a desk to be delivered to her office. Tomorrow afternoon she would ring Debbie and, gradually, judiciously, she would bring her affair with Erich to a close. And then? Then she would be alone with the space in her life that she held apart from Dave, a space as broad as the horizon of this city, with its skyline bereft of landmarks. She could see how Dave would smile at her this evening, his right eyebrow twitching, as she asked him for the loan. "You're part of the company now? I'm telling you, Vivian, you could do anything!"

A SENSE OF TIME

IN THE EARLY stages of a middle age he held at bay by refusing to admit to its onset, Emmett, who worked as an editor in Winnipeg, took a four-month leave of absence in England, where he had completed a graduate degree a dozen years earlier. For two months he made the rounds of London's museums and theatres. Having spent too much money on a short-term rental near Victoria Station, he tried to earn back some of his costs by sending freelance articles on London life to Canadian newspapers. The recurrent theme of these articles, as dictated from editorial desks in Winnipeg, Toronto or Montreal, was that there would always be an England, that Great Britain was a land of fog, eccentrics, double-decker buses and the Royal Family, where nothing changed.

One evening, leafing through the cultural section of a newspaper in search of material, while Turkish music welled through the wall from the next flat, Emmett spotted a small announcement for a conference on the works of a poet who had been born a century earlier. The conference would take place in the rainy town where Emmett had completed his graduate degree. The sight of the name of the building where he had listened to dozens of lectures afflicted him with a pang at not having visited his alma mater. Early on Saturday morning, before the Polish delicatessen on the ground floor had opened for business, he left the building and caught a bus out of London from Victoria Coach Station, got off on the High Street of the rainy town, and made his way to a room where he had taken notes a dozen years before. Among the fifty or so people seated on the hard chairs he recognized half a dozen of his former teachers. His first reaction was of bludgeoned depression before the greying passage of time. The men he remembered as vigorous authorities in their fields were worn and stooped. He re-introduced himself to an intimidating professor he had not known well, mentioning the year in which he had finished his degree. The man's tight face unclenched into a glorious smile. Adopting a more casual approach, Emmett sauntered up to a professor who had supervised one of his research papers. "I know who you are," the man muttered, his bowed head discouraging further conversation. Chastened, Emmett approached the next professor with a circumspect extended hand. The only common denominator among their reactions was their unpredictability. The English, Emmett decided, were the most inscrutable people on earth.

He took a seat as a very elderly professor, who had been retired and venerated even when Emmett was a student, approached the podium to open the proceedings. This professor had taught most of the other professors when they were undergraduates. His small stature was accentuated by the inordinate length of his earlobes, which almost grazed the collar of his blue blazer.

Behind him, the door opened to admit a trickle of latecomers. One of them, an angular Englishwoman in her thirties with curly auburn hair, sat down across the aisle from Emmett

The elderly professor told stories about the poet whose centenary they were celebrating. British academics, some of them younger than Emmett, gave papers on the poet's work. The face of the woman seated across from him niggled at his memory like a mould for a succession of related images; he supposed he had seen many Englishwomen who looked like this.

At the intermission, the professor who had ignored Emmett walked down the aisle as the woman got to her feet. He greeted her and asked her what she was doing. Emmett, standing up, found himself included in their conversation. The professor, with a wave, said: "Cecilia, you know Emmett, don't you?"

"Of course," she said.

Emmett flinched. "I — "

She stared him in the eyes. Her dark-brown incisiveness pinned him from beneath eyebrows of felt-like softness. In her confident upper-class voice, she said: "We know each other from the back reading room."

Memory melted the prominence of her bones until he saw her as she had been at twenty-one: her face rounder, flushed with youthful glory, her hair draped past her shoulders, her body casually fuller than its present disciplined leanness. He wondered how he could have forgotten her. It made him realize that in three or four decades all his experiences would be forgotten; he was ashamed to think that Cecilia had remembered and he had not.

The rest of the intermission was a blur. He barely touched the tea and digestive biscuits on offer at the front of the room. The paper that followed the intermission was the weakest of the day. Emmett's attention wandered; he tried to avoid staring at Cecilia.

He sat across from her at lunch. As she brought the intimidating professor, who was sitting next to her, up to date on her life, he told himself that this information was being unveiled for his benefit. Not only did the English rarely mean what they said, their words were often directed at someone other than the person who they were addressing. Emmett could include this revelation in his next article; it was another way in which England had not changed.

"I went to work for the Foreign Office. It was tremendous fun. They sent me to Chile and to Senegal. Then I met this bloke and we decided to get married. John's a doctor down in Surrey . . . You can't have a marriage where one of you's abroad all the time, so I left the F.O. and now I'm rather at a loose end, which is why I've the time to come here today . . . "

Listening to her voice, replete with its self-assurance that certain sorts of jobs were hers by right, Emmett fell silent. He did not mention that he worked as an editor; it did not seem important. As lunch ended and they walked back to the lecture room along an unheated corridor, Cecilia drew alongside him. "You do remember me now?"

"Yes," he said. "I remember you very well."

They entered the room and sat down. As the afternoon's first speaker began his presentation, Emmett risked a surreptitious glance in the direction of the face that resembled a mask made from the face he recalled. He had been a graduate student in his thirties, solitary and introverted, sunken in the research papers he was writing, yet watchful and curious about British life. Near the end of the academic year, with the approach of the comprehensive exams that were the crescendo of a British undergraduate degree, the library swarmed with students studying for their dreaded "finals." The front room filled up. Other graduate students made themselves scarce; Emmett took refuge in the back reading room. A place of thirty-foot ceilings supported by book-lined walls, the back reading room contained oak tables covered with green baize secured by brass bolts. Emmett claimed a spot at a table beneath a statue of an emaciated-looking 19th-century decadent writer. The young women studying for finals whispered over their bulging notebooks and marked-up editions of classic novels, yet the twitter was less insistent than in the front room. By four or five in the afternoon most of the undergraduates drifted away, leaving Emmett alone; he worked straight through until closing time at seven o'clock. Cecilia, whose name he had not known until today, sat across the table from him with two regular friends and others who came and went. He noticed her enough to recognize her. Tracking his own base masculine reactions with the dulled obsessiveness of prolonged solitude, he wondered at how there were days when she looked teddy-bearish and almost childlike and other days when he found her womanly and mature. In his fantasy life, which was the only life he had at that point, he enshrined her as his mascot. He soon realized that she had noticed his attention. Her recognition was discreet; there were no giggling whispers with her study mates. As finals progressed, the crowds in the library grew more intent on their books. Then the undergraduates began to finish and disappear, and some of Emmett's fellow graduate students returned. Emmett continued to work in the back room. One day he overheard Cecilia's study mate whisper, "Is this your last one?"

"Yes," she said. "Tomorrow morning it's *over*."

Emmett continued working, his head lowered. At five o'clock Cecilia's mates urged her to leave with them. She shook her head. Outside the enormous windows, low clouds grew darker. "If you don't come now you'll get soaked!" her friend whispered. A few minutes later the rain poured down. Emmett and Cecilia, sitting across the table from each other, were alone. The lamp on the table between them was barely strong enough to light the pages of the spiral-bound notebook into which he was copying significant passages from a thick work of literary criticism. A tension gripped him; in the gloom, her body felt so close that he didn't dare look up. He was aware of the indentations that his pencil, pressing through the notebook pages, left in the green baize, the flare of the oak table's sculpted leg pressing into his knee.

The rain ended. Sunlight pierced the clouds, filling the vault-like room with a slanting pre-dusk glow whose golden richness contained only a streak of the coming sunset. The fleeting light embossed the spines of the leather-bound books. When Emmett glanced up, Cecilia had closed her notebook and was looking towards him, not quite meeting his eyes. He looked at her and could not look away. Her cardigan hung over the back of her chair. She was wearing a deep-pink short-sleeved blouse. A ruffle of long hair, straying onto her breast, had been rubbed to an almost russet colour by the rare sunlight that would vanish with the next cloud that passed; the warmth radiated into her face. He could not help but fall towards her. Cecilia trained her eyes just below the level where her gaze would meet his. He took her hand — it felt soft and childish and moist — and, as though their clasp had become the most supple of pivots, levered himself halfway to his feet and slipped around the end of the oak table until he was standing behind her chair with the gaunt statue stretching above him. He slid his hands inside her blouse and down her back. He undid the hook of her bra, then, with a quick upward curl of his palms, he cupped her breasts. He caught her nipples between his thumb and forefinger, caressing them until Cecilia's breathing became audible. She arched her back and looked up over her shoulder, seeking his eyes.

The light dimmed as clouds shifted outside the window; a gash of conversation from the main reading room made their bodies tighten. Cecilia shook herself to her feet. He was startled by the adroitness with which she fastened her bra, adjusted her blouse and shrugged herself into her cardigan. Tossing her hair out of her eyes, she said: "I went to a girls' school. That sort of thing didn't happen much. It hasn't happened much here, either. I think that's just what I needed to set me up for my last final." These were the only words she spoke to him. Before he could reply, she gathered up her books, turned away, then turned back and brushed a clumsy kiss across his cheek. He drew a deep breath, sat down at the table and worked straight through until seven o'clock. He never saw her again.

His desolation at having forgotten this moment bore down on him for the whole afternoon, ruining his concentration.

The conference ended at five o'clock with an invitation from the intimidating professor to meet for the opening of an exhibition of the poet's manuscripts. The ceremony would be held in half an hour's time in a display room of the library.

Emmett stumbled through the crowd. At the doorway he found the venerable professor who had known the poet talking to Cecilia. He dropped into stride alongside them. The three of them walked together down the High Street and across the city centre to the library. Darkness had fallen and the neon logos of the chain stores that had driven away the family businesses Emmett remembered were gleaming in the chill mist that was not quite rain. The smell of diesel fuel, kebabs, curry and fish-and-chips basting in stale oil blended in the fine moist specks that dampened his face. The elderly professor, his hair brushed straight back, walked with a stride whose vigour surprised Emmett. Looking around his outsized earlobes at Cecilia, he said: "And what will you do now, my dear?"

"I think I might have children," Cecilia said.

Emmett thought of suckling infants diminishing her breasts: the only breasts he had ever caressed without seeing what they looked like. As though alerted to his scrutiny, Cecilia asked him: "Are you married?"

"I was married," Emmett said.

"I met my wife here," the elderly professor said. "In fact, I met her in the library. We were both undergraduates. It seems like yesterday. It's difficult to believe that we're over eighty now."

"I have a hard time believing that I'm over thirty," Cecilia said. "Even though I'm married, in a fundamental way nothing seems to have changed in years."

"I can scarcely believe this chap we've spent the whole day discussing isn't among us any more," the professor said, his voice rasping. "When I met him he was a very robust man . . . You know, my dear, if you do have children you will feel that things have changed. You'll have . . . "

"A sense of time passing?" Emmett suggested, as they approached the steps of the library.

"Yes," the professor said. "Precisely that."

The reception bored him. There was wine and cheese and a short, dull speech; self-congratulatory cliques pursued academic politics under the guise of socializing. After twenty minutes of staring at the manuscripts preserved in air-tight display cases, Emmett decided to catch the next bus back to London. He found Cecilia topping up her wine. "I'm leaving," he murmured.

"I'll walk you to the door." With a giggle, she said: "You know . . . the other time . . . I never heard you speak. I didn't realize you were from abroad."

"Would that have made a difference?" Emmett asked as they stepped out of the display room. They avoided looking at the marble staircase leading to the reading rooms.

"It would have made it more unbearable." Her breath came in a rush. They were outside, the mist brushing their faces as the shadow-folded half-light of the broad front steps enveloped them. "That day in the back reading room left me in a rage," she whispered. "After finals I got a job and a flat in London and I shagged the first bloke I met. That day got me started on my career with men." Laying her fingertips on his shoulders, she kissed him on the mouth. He moaned at the deftness of her tongue. As his legs began to tremble, she pulled away. "That's all you get. That's what I owed you that day, a really good snog — if only I'd known how."

"It's nice to be repaid after all these years." His heart was thrumming. In a gesture that felt foolish, he offered her his Winnipeg business card. "Let me know when your baby is born. Or," lowering his voice, "tell me if the old professor dies."

"I'll do that," Cecilia said. "I'll be happy to keep you up to date."

Without speaking or touching, they turned away. Emmett closed his eyes; the mist made his eyelids damp. He knew that, one way or the other, he would hear from her again.

FREEDOM SQUARE

Her mother's hands closed around her wrist. "You're not leaving us?"

"Yes. I got the job. It's only for the summer."

"A whole summer. When I was a student I was allowed to go to Paris for two weeks. Two weeks made me a French teacher." Two years ago, when Doina was finishing at the *liceu*, her father and mother had told her she could plan to attend university in Bucharest because they had money for the train fare. "Your cousin Rodica will be going to Cluj," her mother said. "Her parents can't pay for her to travel to Bucharest and back four times a year." Since then pity had flowed between them in one direction only. Hearing the news, Doina had felt the first hunch of resentment, knowing that her mother not only had studied in Bucharest but had grown up there. Doina must feel guilty not only for the privileges which she could take for granted and her mother had been denied, but also for the privileges they shared; she must even feel guilty for the advantages her mother had enjoyed over her.

Her mother's grip slid from her wrist to her forearm. "Hold me while I put my boots on." Doina watched her sock foot swab a damp patch on the tiles where her father had brushed snow off the heavy coat he wore to the mine. When her mother was dressed they went outside. Snow covered the mountains; water from this morning's rain lay in the streets. The misty air pricked her cheeks, sifting clouds down over the single-storey stucco bungalows and the yards where mud was breaking through the snow. "If you spend the summers in Germany," her mother said, "you won't get to know people in Bucharest."

"I don't care about Bucharest. It's like here. People just throw things on the ground, they never repair the streets."

"You'll come to care for it. You can have a cultured life there."

Doina paused, evaluating this appeal, which acknowledged her longings but misunderstood them. "I don't know if I'm looking for culture," she said in a slow voice. "I think I'm looking for beauty."

"You're lucky that you're studying design. If you were studying literature or history or mathematics you would have your four years in Bucharest, then you would be assigned a job as a teacher in some village and that would be your life."

"Like what happened to you."

"This is not a village. It is a city — "

"An ugly city. All mines and metallurgic plants."

"You grew up in a house, not a socialist flat. You have had privileges and opportunities — "

"That you never had. Yes, I know."

The muddy water gushing under the bridge silenced them as they entered the old city. They walked beneath the Gothic towers, past the remnants of the 15th-century walls, the monument to Jews deported during the Holocaust. Doina knew that through an innate reverse logic both she and her mother were thinking by contrast of the rest of the city: the faceless tower block apartment buildings, the metallurgic plants as large as medieval city-states dominating the plain below the mountains. She remembered Ceauşescu's time, which had ended before she was ten: the evenings so long and silent that even the two hours' daily television programming about the dictator's accomplishments became fascinating. Her father had just become a manager at the mine. He looked nervous as her mother tried to tune in Western radio stations in French or English. The power cuts sabotaged her mother's plans to convert Doina to French literature; from childhood she felt closer to English than French, closer to pictures than words. The shapeless overcoat of the dictator's wife hung in her imagination after the two hours of television had ended, the stodgy lines demanding to be redrawn. All night she dreamed of tight hems, splayed collars and stylish pockets. In the morning she woke to the peasant toilet built onto the back of the bungalow, a cold shower, the smog-cover that broke only when icy January gales swooped down from the mountains, the tired hue of her skin. The smog had dispersed in recent years, as filtered smokestacks had replaced decrepit ones, but to forgive the offence the city had made to her childhood would be to forgive her mother, and that she could never do.

They entered the irregular oblong perfection of Freedom Square. Conscious that the square's medieval jigsawed symmetry offered what Doina rated as the city's only valid aesthetic experience, her mother renewed her challenge. "But you could live in Bucharest! I never thought my family would be able to return — "

"Did you ever think anyone in your family would be able to work in Germany for the summer? Why can't you be proud of that?" When she looked up from the melting snow to press her question, her mother's dark eyes were already foreign.

"You don't look like your mother," Hans said. Doina felt foolish for having shown him these marred prints, the shabby portfolio she had lugged on the train across Hungary and Austria to Munich as though afraid the studio that had hired her might change its mind unless she arrived with tangible proof of her abilities. She felt particularly foolish for having included a portrait of her mother among her studies of Freedom Square at dusk and peasants' log houses in the mountains. Hans said she was like an *Ossi*, insecure and trying too hard. The dangerous awareness that this urge to try too hard had contributed to her willingness to sleep with the boss's son tingled between them across the sheets of his bed. Hans had his own flat, bought for him by his parents, on the top floor of a building that faced south towards the Alps. Her second Saturday in Germany he had driven her down the Autobahn for a boat ride across the lake known as the Chiemsee. As the mountains took on a festive air alien to the glowering hulks of overgrown hills at home, Hans curled his arm around her shoulder. She liked his big square body and the pale blue eyes that made her skin feel appreciated by a softer light than any she had been subjected to in Romania. She laughed at how, still a good Catholic son at twenty-seven, he left her dozing among the sheets on Sunday morning to accompany his parents to Mass and Sunday lunch. She let herself out with the key he had given her and returned to the attic room above the studio that came with her job.

"My mother comes from a different world."

Hans fingered the edge of the photograph, whose flaws were so much more evident to her than they had been to the anxious girl who had packed her portfolio to travel west. "She is your mother so she is older than you, but even so you are not looking similar." They were speaking English, their common language. She had worried that her three years of English at *liceu* would not get her through the summer, but the problem scarcely arose. "She is not in the same *frame*," Hans said. He laughed; his fingers stroked her stomach. She rolled over and ruffled his straight blond hair. As Hans set aside the photograph to embrace her, she wallowed in his ability to identify *her* as the source of the beauty she sought. Her boyfriends at *liceu* and during her first year of university had not revealed this possibility to her. She exulted in his recognition of the differences between her and her mother. Rodica liked to say that they did not look like mother and daughter — her mother small and broad-faced with glossy black eyebrows, Doina tall, almost Italian in appearance, her hair a hive of natural curls — but until now no one had given these differences the significance Doina felt they deserved.

After they had made love, Hans said: "There is pain in your mother's face."

"Her back hurts her. She must wear a brace." The last word, which she knew in English, was unfamiliar to Hans. She explained it to him. He stared at the ceiling, his fingers resting on her hip.

"I have thought it was from Communism. You are seeing it in the faces of the old *Ossis*. If you go to Dresden, to Leipzig. They have had hard lives."

"My mother's back started to hurt only after Ceauşescu's time ended. She has had a better life than many people."

In the moments when Hans disappointed her she grasped that he resembled his parents. Herr and Frau Mauer planned each hour of her work schedule. She could not slip out of the studio to shop for cosmetics or spend her first Deutschmarks having her eyebrows trimmed. The Mauers ate lunch at work. A tall, effusive, dark-haired girl named Gabi brought in sandwiches on heavy black bread. Gabi never failed to give Doina a friendly wave. One day, when Doina tried out a few words of German on her, Gabi laughed and touched her elbow. She would gossip for a minute, issue a resounding, *"Auf Wiedersehen!"* to Herr and Frau Mauer, pat Hans on the shoulder, then leave. Unable to digest the black bread, the one time that she tried it, Doina asked to go out for lunch. She needed the break. As she was unable to serve customers in German, she spent most of her day in the dark room. Later in the summer, she was invited into discussions on cropping and mounting and choosing backgrounds and frames. Her flare for design caught Herr Mauer's eye, as her lean body continued to hold the attention of his son. She spied disapproval and opportunism in the father's gaze as he said: "Our gypsy girl is good with colours." She had learned that it was pointless trying to explain that not everyone from Romania was a gypsy. By this time she understood enough to stand in the background during discussions with clients and occasionally suggest a change in simple German. The strictness of Hans's parents discouraged her from venturing farther into the thickets of their language.

She thought she had misunderstood when Frau Mauer, at the beginning of August, told her that she would have a holiday because the studio would close for one day. "After this day," Frau Mauer said, in her difficult English, "we must all very hard work. Hans is not here for three weeks."

"Hans is not here?"

"No, he is married and then . . . to Italy for *die Hochzeitsreise!*"

She felt herself evaporating. She did not exist. She gripped the counter: her tensed clutch crept up her spine. She whispered: "With who is he marrying?"

"*Mit der Verlobte, natürlich*. A wonderful girl, very good Catholic parents. You know Gabi, who brings us *Schwarzbrot* and comes to lunch with us on Sundays after Mass?"

Only days later did she reflect on the composure with which she succeeded in shaking her head, leaving the front of the studio and shutting herself in the dark room before she burst into tears. It seemed like a good sign then, this ability to control her feelings; but for the next few days it was bare emotion, not her ability to contain it, that rivetted her. She saw Gabi's breeziness as condescension, as evidence of superficiality undergirded by a crippling adherence to rules. She and Hans barely touched when Gabi came around with lunch. When were they together? At formal Sunday lunch with Hans's parents! No wonder Hans longed to sleep with an anxious girl from the east. From the first gust of squashed tears that overspilled her hands as she pressed them into her face in the stifling air of the dark room, she felt her anger pouring towards Gabi. Rage against Hans, though she summoned it again and again, refused to rise up in her heart. She fantasized about coming downstairs at night, when she was alone in the building, destroying the studio and blaming the destruction on Gabi. She gazed around the vacant floors and counters, all clean lines and empty space, struggling to accept that this was Germany, this was her life. For the first time in months, she felt a headache coming on. She turned on the computer next to the case displaying film, accessed her hotmail account and wrote a long, furious email to Rodica. She deleted the message unsent, and wrote a second message, which still sounded too shrill the next day when she reread it at the bottom of Rodica's reply. *Don't be a fool!* Rodica wrote. She was working for the summer in a pizza parlour in the student district up the hill from the centre of Cluj; Doina thought she knew from which creaking-floored, smoke-filled internet café Rodica was sending her response. *There are some things we must put up with because of where we come from. Has a boy never treated you badly before?*As she sent Rodica a quick note of thanks, she wondered whether her mother had ever had to contend with this form of hardship. The subject of her mother's life before she met her father was off limits; yet on graduation from university her mother had obtained a posting to a city, however remote and polluted, rather than an isolated village, an achievement that must have involved exercising influence on someone. A contradictory current of strength flowed through Doina as this thought crossed her mind. She made her way to the toilet with discreet steps and washed her face, emerging dazzled by the bright sunlight cutting through the glass front of the studio. That evening after work she trailed through the city, hating its excessive cleanliness, its sharp glowing edges.

The tears returned when she went back to the studio and shut the door of her attic room. She promised herself that she would get what she wanted from Herr and Frau Mauer, just as Gabi had done.

At the end of the third week, when Hans came into work, she waited until he was alone in the dark room, then stepped inside and handed him the spare key. "Now I do not need this." The guilt that spread over his round obedient face gave her all the revenge she required. She cut off his effort to explain. "We must work together, so it is better if you do not say anything stupid." The phrase came out with more bitterness than she had intended. A jab of irritation quickened her step as she left the dark room.

She learned every detail of the studio's work. Herr Mauer sent her on shoots around Munich, paying for her blue striped card so she could ride the U-Bahn to flats that were for sale and take the photographs that would appear in the real estate agent's portfolio. He was stern in his criticism. "You do not frame your photographs properly. Your angles are too wide. If you show the whole flat in one shot, people do not look closely enough at its strong points." They were communicating in a mixture of English and German now, a hybrid patter she achieved with no one else. Hans, who spoke to her in undiluted English, looked on in frustration. Doina preferred the rough-and-tumble effect she created with her wide angles, but for Herr Mauer she learned precision, becoming adept at framing each feature in its rectangle. At the end of the summer, when Hans was taking a week off to move into his large new flat with Gabi, Herr Mauer said: "Will our gypsy girl come back next summer?"

She returned to Bucharest with a wad of Deutschmarks big enough to allow her to pay her own train fares. She went home to see her parents, fending off their envy; she stopped in Cluj to see Rodica and repelled her envy; she returned to her design studies and envied the literature students who were learning flawless English, German or French. By the next summer she was shattered by Bucharest's grimy mediocrity, the soulless emptiness of Unity Square, the debasement of the fine old buildings around University Square into neon-drenched casinos with thugs in black tuxedos patrolling the doorways. In November she slept with a well-off Bucharest boy in order, she told herself, to get Hans out of her system. Her single night's impulse turned into months of agony. The boy's dark eyes knew her too well; no allusion or turn of phrase escaped his tireless analytical energy. When he derided her home in the provinces, he did so with a knowledge that made his words hurtful in a way that Hans's remarks about *Ossis* never had been. She rode the train home for Christmas through a landscape of snowed-in poor country huts, the frozen washing hanging flat as planks on lines strung across the barren yards, until the smokestacks heaved into view. Her mother knew that her moodiness must be related to a boy, a perception that made Doina feel more miserable for being predictable. By April, when she finally succeeded in shaking herself free, she felt overwhelmed by ugliness: the ugliness of the city, the ugliness of her mind, incapable of conceiving the lines demanded by her year-end project, the ugliness of her face, puffy from tears and headaches and sleeplessness. She told her mother over the phone of her decision to return to Germany.

"Is that where he is, the boy who was troubling you at Christmas?"

"No, Mama. I can earn good money there, that's all. How are you? Is your back hurting?"

The line went still. "This summer," her mother said, "I am going to reread all of Proust. Think of me reading Proust while you take photographs."

There was little more to say. She felt relieved when the train stopped in Munich and pale blue eyes, or even brown eyes, saw nothing more in her than a girl from the east. She guarded her damaged vision of beauty in her chest, holding it close to her like an infant at the breast. When she got off the tram at the photo studio Hans greeted her with a hearty, nervous handshake. "You are lucky!" he boomed. "My father is going to send you all over Europe. It would cost a lot to send one of us, but you are cheap!"

Herr Mauer had won a contract to supply photographs for brochures of holiday flats in Italy and the south of France. Doina took the photographs, framing each attribute of every flat in a suitable rectangle. After her first trip to Italy she began to carry a second camera to take wild, ragged shots of the *piazza* of each perfect little town, developing the prints in secret in the dark room at night. The summer filled up with air and light and warmth and buoyancy. She sent her mother postcards from Nice and Cannes, risking a few words of faulty French above her name. She expected Italian to be close enough to Romanian that she would understand it without effort, and was surprised at how little she could make out. Twice that summer she took advantage of the opportunities she discovered travelling alone, knowing there was little danger of strangers perceiving anything about her that she did not wish to reveal. These nights with Italian men helped her fix herself in the beauty she saw around her; her Bucharest winter ugliness receded. Nowhere, she was certain, could match Italy for beauty. Yet it was a beauty she could not transport or share, or even understand; she could take home her Euros — the new currency was another change this summer had brought — and her photographs of Italian squares more wonderful than Freedom Square in their impulsive yet unerring sense of proportion. After two summers of travelling on Herr Mauer's behalf, she returned to Romania with a thick pile of Euros. Her design degree was finished, exempting her from ever returning to Bucharest. She would look for work in Cluj, the closest Romanian city to the West, where Renault, Nissan and other Western companies were establishing their toeholds in the old east, and according to Rodica, the best city in which to meet boys. Rodica, who was moving to London to work illegally, offered Doina her flat. Doina rode the train home to tell her mother of her decision. A tailings dam had burst and cyanide-contaminated water had spilled into the river. As they crossed the bridge into the old city, the carcasses of dead fish floated on the dark green water like faded sheaths. "What will you do in Cluj?" her mother asked.

"Make beauty here in this ugly country."

"Basing yourself on what? A few photographs?"

"What do you know? You never leave this polluted city." Doina felt irritation wrapping itself around her brain. This was her second headache in a week.

"I carry Proust with me wherever I go. What do you carry?"

Doina tried to draw breath; her lungs felt empty. She narrowed her eyes and watched her mother's tight-hipped steps. Sensing her advantage, her mother turned to insist on an answer. "I don't know," Doina said, weakened by the pounding in her head, which she knew would pursue her for the rest of her life. "I don't know anything! But I haven't left. I'm staying here. Isn't that more than you expected?"

NOTHING WISHES TO BE DIFFERENT

Nimic nu vrea să fie altfel decît este.
(Nothing wishes to be different than it is.)
— Lucian Blaga

LITTLE BOYS SELLING raspberries in slender paper packets surrounded Lucian on the wooden platform. He watched the dark blue train climbing mountain meadows past cabins with fertility emblems over their doors. To the boys he was a tall, funny old man with hair as thick as a sheep's fleece. He had hemmed the cuffs and pockets of his orange shirt with white thread. Last year, brooding that he had never seen the sea, he had realized that fishermen were no less manly because they did their own sewing. He decided to darn his socks and shirts himself rather than sending them to a widow. A widow who sewed for him might make other claims, and that would upset his children.

He had remained faithful to Alina throughout their marriage. It was a source of comfort to him now, but it had been a torment at the time. As a tall, athletic young veterinarian, he had felt Satan torturing him with the thick hair, long tight thighs and taut breasts of women who knelt next to him. It was a gift from God that he had only once caressed another woman's breasts.

Lucian climbed into the train and found his compartment. In the sloping fields men and women stooked hay into tall, gleaming cones. He had been a child when the farthest peaks on the opposite side of the valley had become Romanian after the First World War, and a defeated soldier when the peaks had been lost to the Soviet Union. By the time the creation of an independent Ukraine had made it possible once again to travel to the mountain village over the border where his mother had been born, he was an old man. Doubting he could endure the long journey to his mother's village, he had decided on a different destination for his trip.

The journey to Stalingrad had begun on a train. He could barely remember the night before their departure, when they had visited the prostitutes. The memory that persisted was of his unbalanced feeling the next morning as they tramped into the troop wagon. His shoulders felt aslant beneath the weight of his pack. As a boy in his village Lucian had made love with a girl next to a river at night. He loved this girl's smile, the sweep of her thick dark hair as cool as mist on his stomach; in the chill of the troop wagon the memory of her made him want to moan.

The prostitutes waited for the soldiers in narrow wooden beds permeated with the smell of candle wax and sweat. His comrades' groaning broke through the blankets slung over lengths of hemp to separate the beds. He had not known that the act of love could be emptied of love, the body moving forward without the spirit. When their officers spoke of the need to defeat Oriental Bolshevism Lucian imagined Bolsheviks as bodies without spirits, men whose flesh was pinched in an embrace devoid of love.

On the Eastern Front they rounded up men in the woods and marched across abandoned furrows that reached to the horizon. The villages they entered were inhabited by women and children. The officers ordered the younger women to sleep with them; enlisted men foraged among the leftovers. The women bowed their heads when chosen by a soldier. Knowing their husbands were unlikely to return, they proved more welcoming in bed. Only the Romanians fell in love. Lucian observed in his compatriots a deep gash of sentiment lacking in the German, Hungarian and Croatian soldiers advancing into Russia: each encounter with a woman was awash in emotion. He fell in love three times. The worst time was with a Kazakh woman with a large nose and thick eyebrows that turned as soft as black lambswool beneath the moonlight. They spoke in broken German; he felt their closeness seize him like the grip of moss on stone. For two weeks they slept together naked beneath sheepskin blankets. In the morning she brought him goat's milk warm from the nanny's teat. At Stalingrad, when the Russian tanks counter-attacked through the fog hanging over the endless snow, Lucian remembered her as the last woman he would touch.

The bunkers of Dumitrescu's Third Army collapsed beneath the Russian artillery fire, burying his comrades. Lucian ran. To his amazement, he did not die. Every man he knew was buried or shot or captured and sent to starve in Siberia. Lucian dodged between two tanks, let the fog cover him and threw himself into a retreating German train. When spring came, he deserted his bivouac in the German camp where he had stolen cabbages to stay alive. He went in search of the village where he had fallen in love. He walked over the plains of scorched, roofless houses, trampled gardens, caved-in stone walls, sheds empty of animals, fields barren of crops. He slept out in the cold and drank rain water caught in his cupped hands to spare himself from dysentery. Two months later, bearded and nearly starving, he was picked up by a straggling Romanian platoon and marched back to Romania with them.

He was demobilized in Bucharest, a hot southern city that, even after a war and an earthquake, felt as alien as America. The streets appeared too wide for mere humans, the gleaming windows of the French pastry shops were impossibly long. The people looked like Turks and Gypsies and Bulgarians all rolled into one yet, in contrast to the mountains of Bucovina, he heard only Romanian spoken. Lucian missed the sounds of German and Ukrainian. He remembered his grandfather, who had thought of himself first as an Austro-Hungarian and only after as a Romanian. Even his mother had never believed in the Greater Romania of the interwar years. Now they lived in a shrivelled Romania, a Sovietized Romania. Where had all these Communists come from? Before the war he knew only young men like himself, who believed in God and in Romania's glorious destiny. Bolshevism had been a Russian illness; he had trusted in God to strike it down. His memories of Stalingrad continued to disturb him. How had the Bolsheviks held out against the combined might of the Christian armies, continuing to fight after even the city's rats and leather belts had been eaten? If they were men without souls, where had they found the strength to outlast a siege by men who prayed to God? Shaken, he kept quiet during the Communist takeover. He told his demobilization committee that he was a shepherd's son from Bucovina who had followed his country's calling during the war and looked forward to helping to rebuild Romania in peace. They sent him to veterinary college. He read and wrote well enough to take notes during the animal anatomy lectures; blessed with a good memory, he passed his exams without difficulty. He met Alina in a cinema, where the shadow of her broad-nosed profile made him start. He went over to speak to her and felt himself longing to caress her beneath a rough blanket. They were married six months later. Lucian was assigned to work in the market, examining animals to certify their health before they were sold. The manager, a hunched man known as Mircea the Old, had been a member of the Communist Party since the 1920s. "You believe in God," he said, his gnarled right hand splayed like a cloven hoof across the rail of a livestock pen. "Men who believed in God tortured me. They ruined my hand."

"If they tortured you," Lucian said, "they were not Christians."

Mircea the Old snorted. "I could have you imprisoned. But if you do your job and keep your beliefs to yourself we can get along."

Religion, though he practised it in secret, became the core of his life. He taught his children their prayers as soon as they were able to speak. Alina taught them that prayers were uttered only in their apartment, in the presence of Mama and Tata. They must be kept secret from playmates. Having grown up in a hilltop village where no one had seen an electric light, Alina revelled in their two-bedroom apartment with heat, electricity and running water. "You shouldn't be so critical of the Communists, Lucian. Thanks to them, we're giving our children comforts we never had. They let me leave my job each time I have a child, and when I'm ready to return my job is waiting for me."

Leaning around the corner of the children's bedroom, Lucian looked at the three small bodies lying side by side: two in wooden cots, the youngest still in a crib. The birth of his children had turned him into a more cautious man. He kept to himself on the morning tram-ride to the market. He acceded to his wife's wishes in family decisions, recognizing that the children's welfare was her first concern. Every summer the government offered them the choice of *munţi sau mare* for their vacation. Mircea the Old, he knew, chose not to take vacations: giving up his privileges was his contribution to building socialism. Though Lucian dreamed of watching his children frolic on Black Sea beaches, he acquiesced with Alina's belief that hiking in the mountains was healthier. The cool evenings in the mountain stations north of Bucharest — Sinaia, Bucegi, Poiana Braşov — raised faint memories of Bucovina. Standing next to Alina as they watched the two older children stumble up a rocky slope, he said: "Perhaps next year we can go to Constanţa."

"Lucian, I don't want to spend my vacation afraid that the children may drown. Look at how they love the mountains!"

The revelation came at the end of a day spent examining sheep. He was lying on his bed, neither awake nor asleep, listening to the sounds of Alina making supper. The light was off. And then the room was filled with light. Not an electric light but a pure glimmering, a ray so pristine that a single drop expanded into a vast, translucent space. The garlicky smell of

Alina's *ciorbă de burta* vanished. He felt himself enveloped in sweetness. A celestial breath lifted him off the bed. A man of one hundred kilos, he was suspended in the air amid the promise of eternal life. For a few moments he floated among the angels as he might do one day in Heaven. The sweetness intoxicated him with a blissful innocence that deepened his sight. He trembled, terrified by his failure to announce to all his faith in God.

When Alina came to call him for supper he was staring at the ceiling with tears in his eyes.

"What's the matter?"

He sat up, shaking his head.

During supper she looked at him over her soup while she urged the children to fill themselves up on bread. That night, when they were alone, she said: "What were you thinking about?"

"Stalingrad." He told her again about the siege. She accepted that a man who had fought in the war would need to talk about it more than once. It was true that Stalingrad had wounded him. The resistance of the bodies without spirits had driven his faith underground. He had continued to observe the Orthodox fast on Friday, eating only food that came from the earth. But his visits to church were rare and furtive. Without his noticing it, his faith was trickling away.

He had been commanded to act. Suspicious of the Orthodox patriarchs, notorious for their collaboration with the government, he visited one of the men who had marched back to Bucharest with him. It took Lucian six months to earn the man's trust. One morning he kissed Alina and his children, boarded the tram to work and stayed on two stops past the market. He climbed into the back of a truck and allowed the lid of a feed vat to be fastened over his head. Eighteen hours later he was home in Bucovina. Two days after that he was in a mountain camp with a stolen Soviet carbine in his hands.

During his months in the mountains he often depended on charity. The people of the country's northern fringes were as generous as they were stubborn. Remorseless collectivization of the land had faltered on the flanks of the northern mountains. The villages were remote, the terrain steep and forbidding. Hostile to any notion originating more than a day's walk away, the villagers felled trees across the muddy roads when they heard that Communist Party officials were on their way. Religious men defying Communism were greeted with *mamaligă*, bowls of soup, a chicken or a lamb shank. Lucian repaid the peasants with advice on the health of their sheep and goats. For eighteen months his renegade guerrilla unit, disowned by the church hierarchy, tweaked the government's tail. They helped the peasants fell trees across roads. When soldiers were sent to clear the trees, Lucian's men attacked their makeshift barracks, blowing up their trucks and jeeps. They fled into the woods to camouflaged camps high in the mountains. For them the war had not ended: they were continuing the battle that had begun when the Soviet tanks had advanced against the besiegers of Stalingrad.

The longer Lucian remained in the mountains the more his years in Bucharest felt like self-deception. He missed his children, but he knew he had come home. The peasants' cottages reminded him of his childhood. Yet, after so many years away, they were also strange: the heathen fertility emblems he used to know by heart irritated him. These people would never be pure Christians, just as they would never be Communists.

During the winter they suspended their campaign. They shot a hibernating bear and moved into its cave. When they had eaten the last bear-steak and snow had drifted across the cave's mouth, the youngest man was sent down the mountain. He returned with permission from the monks to move into an abandoned wooden monastery in a clearing near a tall peak. From the monastery's balcony they could survey the valley down a chute of snow so long and steep that the forests below resembled patches of flat moss. Taking his turn on watch, Lucian imagined that this whiteness was the ocean. In moments when he missed Alina he concentrated on the light that would envelope him when his life ended. The promise of glorious sweetness urged him on. All winter they stockpiled weapons, planning their spring offensive. The boxes of ammunition glowed beneath the roof of the monastery.

The government was consolidating its presence in the region by building a lumberyard and a mill. The mill would offer regular wages; small apartment blocks would be built next to the lumberyard to house workers and their families. The promise of running water and electricity would draw men off their ancestral plots. Once the peasants had left their land, it would be collectivized. At four o'clock on a spring morning, after fervent prayers, Lucian and his comrades attacked the mill with hand grenades. They knocked down the metal fence. Lucian rushed through the gap while his comrades remained poised to cover him. In the darkness he saw the white ends of the logs peering at him like the stacked eyes of owls. He heard the guards shouting. One of them began firing from the door of the hut where they slept. As they opened the door and scanned the yard with their flashlights, they became perfect targets. Lucian shot them both through the chest. He hurried across the springy, woodchip-covered earth and shot the man lying closest to him through the temple. The second man's body shuddered at the impact. "*Dumnezeu*," he moaned. "*Dumnezeu* . . . "

"You believe in God?" Lucian said. His shoulder ached from the rifle's recoil.

The man curled up like an infant, a rattling audible in his throat. His flashlight lay before his face, its beam glaring against his brow in contorted self-interrogation. Kicking the flashlight aside to prevent it from being stained with blood, Lucian shot the man through the back of the head.

His comrades slipped out of the darkness. They burned down the mill and the lumberyard, and dynamited the foundations of the apartment blocks. Then they scattered, having arranged to take separate routes to a mountain hideout. They would meet again in five days' time.

The weather turned clear and mild. The first night Lucian slept in the shed of a peasant he had befriended. The peasant's seventeen-year-old daughter never failed to smile at him. In the middle of the night he was awoken by her whispering. The whispers turned to soft laughter as he touched her hand. Lucian kissed the girl and stroked her breasts until he felt her nipples perking up like newborn lambs. He reminded himself of his marriage vows. As the girl's hand slid down his thigh, he nudged her away. "God does not want — "

"If God were alive like us," the girl said, her blue, Slavic-looking eyes edged with pain, "he would not deny himself."

She left. In the morning, bringing him bread and cheese for breakfast, she looked at the dirt floor.

"Why won't you look at me?"

"Because you don't think I'm pretty."

"I think you are pretty but I am a married man." He saw her shoulders straighten, lifting her light brown hair out of her eyes. "I cannot fight for God and spit in God's face."

As he turned away from the farm, he felt exhilarated. He had been equal to God's test! He hiked all day through the trees, climbing the mountainside to the top of an enormous ridge that ran northward into Trans-Carpathia where, if he kept walking, he would find the village where his mother had been born. The Soviet border made such a trek impossible, yet treading the long spine of the mountains, he delighted in the magical balance between earth and sky. In the morning he had been walking through tall forests where his feet rustled last year's dead leaves. By noon the slopes were so steep that he had to walk bent forward. Farms, peasants and dogs vanished. He walked beneath the cover of coniferous trees that clutched the earth between the jutting rocks. In the early afternoon, reaching the top of the ridge, he broke into the open, unafraid of being spotted as he ambled across the green meadows. Approaching the rock-hemmed edge of the ridge he looked down on clouds. In the rents between the clouds he could see the green valley floor interrupted by dark knots of towns. He was staring down on the world from Heaven. That night, taking advantage of the mild weather, he slept in the open. He lay on his back with his pack beneath his head. The flashlight he had taken from the guard made an uncomfortable bulge. He removed it and laid it next to his ear. Heaven hung so near to him that if he reached out with his arm he would scratch the stars. Earth beneath him, Heaven above, his body stretched empty of unruly desires between them: never before had his existence been summarized with such clarity.

He wished he could always sleep on the top of the ridge. The next morning, as he continued his hike northward, he was stopped by a platoon of soldiers. Sceptical of his story that he was going to visit an ailing uncle in a village near the Soviet border, they searched his pack. The Cyrillic lettering on the guard's flashlight condemned him. Three days later he was transported to Gherla.

As they brought him to the prison, the high ridge of its front wall dominating the small town with its ramshackle streets and dishevelled corn patches, he prepared himself to face interrogation by the secret police. The guards turned him over to children. The students, dressed in the pale pyjamas of psychiatric patients, wore identical convict haircuts. Their faces were soft. They approached him with bewildered expressions that turned to panic and hatred. They beat the soles of his feet for hours. They clubbed his buttocks and his thighs; they beat his balls until they swelled up into hard blue potatoes. They pulled a black hood over his head and smashed his skull against the floor. He held his head for days, groaning. His vision blurred. He vomited until his guts were sore. Each time they returned him to the interrogation room the two uniformed guards stood next to the door in silence while the students swarmed over him. Sometimes three or four of them would beat different parts of his body at once. When they looked him in the eyes, he stared straight through them. They were bodies without souls; he could never match their fury.

He understood how the defenders of Stalingrad had turned back the Christian armies.

After six months the beatings stopped. His interrogations, though they sometimes still involved torture, were conducted by men who sat behind bright lamps and asked him the names of his co-conspirators. They recited his acts of sabotage, surprising him with details he had not expected them to know. One of his interrogators — the polite one, whose job was to win his confidence — told him that the students were dissidents who had been psychologically reconstructed into a state where they were panting to torture fellow dissidents. "An intriguing experiment," the man said. "But the program has been discontinued."

After he told them everything he knew, the interrogations ceased. He was a prisoner: nothing more. His cell was a narrow rectangle with a high ceiling and no window. It contained a cot, a blanket and a bucket. In winter, wrapped in the blanket, he shivered. One spring Gherla flooded and he had to stand on his cot for two days while murky water slurped around his ankles. He forced himself to keep standing by dreaming of the sea. He would watch sun-bright water breaking on the beach where his children swam.

By the time the flood receded the weaker prisoners had died. Unable to remain standing, they had lain down on their cots and drowned. Their bodies were rolled into the wide corridor dividing the rows of cells. The prisoners were released from their cells in pairs to drag away the bodies. Lucian was teamed with a frail old man whose broken right hand could barely grasp the dead man's wrist. As they hauled on the cadaver, the old man said: "Don't you recognize me, Lucian? You put me here."

Mircea the Old had become ancient. His waist was as thin as a broomhandle. The flesh had been scraped from beneath his slackened face. "What are you doing here?" Lucian whispered. "You're one of them."

"Because of you they didn't believe me." Mircea gasped as they dragged the body around a corner. A truck had backed up to the door. Its exhaust pipe pumped fumes into the corridor. "That's what I get for my charity. After you disappeared, they held me responsible. I should have reported you the first time you prated about God."

"I didn't think — "

"You didn't think about me. And look at your wife and children."

"What about my wife and children?"

"Stop talking!" the guard said. They had reached the truck. They pushed the body onto the pile of corpses. The dead man's curled right leg snagged around another corpse's stiffened arm. They pushed until they sweated. The dead man lunged onto the top of the pile. Lucian realized how weak he had become. One of the corpses belched, unleashing a vomit-like smell that made Lucian double over.

A guard straightened him up with a jab of his rifle butt. "Back to your cells!"

Lucian looked in the direction of Mircea the Old. Mircea ignored him as they took him away.

Lucian's cell stank. He prayed for hours, kneeling on the moist silt the flood had deposited on the floor. He had always acted according to the vision that God had sent him. On his second-last night of freedom he had renounced the temptation of making love with a beautiful girl. He could feel the shape of her breasts filling his palms. Though he had regretted ten thousand times not having taken advantage of this last opportunity to make love as a man in his prime, he knew that by refusing he had fulfilled God's design. It was as God's emissary that he had left his family, and as God's instrument that he had shot the Communist guard who remembered his faith in his dying moments. Mircea the Old's imprisonment, too, formed part of God's plan. Everything, Lucian thought, must be as it is. He himself was in Gherla for a reason. His body was growing thinner and weaker for a reason. Nothing could wish to be different. That night, as he closed his eyes on his sodden cot, he remembered his final night of freedom, poised between Heaven and Earth. He felt the grass growing beneath his back.

They released him in 1959. He weighed fifty-seven kilos, a little more than half his weight when he was imprisoned. He was assigned to work on a collective farm in Oltenia. For the first month he slept in a barn. The heat sapped him; he had less strength than a boy of ten. One day the foreman told him he was moving to a cabin. When he reached the door he found the cabin occupied by a large-nosed woman with grey hair and three surly adolescents.

It took him a long time to accept that this was his family.

Alina would not speak to him. The children were tall, strong, yet taciturn. He looked at them one by one. Ion, named after Lucian's father, had Alina's face. He was a gruff, severe boy, almost fifteen. Irina, who was fourteen, followed her mother in everything. He understood that as long as silence persisted between him and his wife, he would hear little from his daughter. Radu, the youngest, was a lively boy who did not remember their apartment in Bucharest. He spoke in a slippery Oltenian dialect, using the literary past tense. When Lucian cocked his head to listen to him, Radu would smile. Then his smile faltered and he hurried away.

His children were not as devout as he had hoped, but he could see that Alina had brought them up well. They were diligent at school, they helped their mother with her chores, they worked on the collective farm. One night as he and Alina lay side by side on the bed without touching he said: "You've done a good job with them."

"Someone had to. Their father thought other things were more important."

"If we could have changed the life of the country," he whispered, barely daring to utter the words even in the blackness of the rural night, "the life of my family would have changed as well."

"After all that's happened," Alina said, "how can you still be a dreamer?"

He felt relieved that they were beginning to talk.

It took him a year of regular meals and work in the fields to approach his former weight. Three months into the year he felt his body growing alert to women's flesh, yet he held off from reaching for Alina until he was certain she would receive him. When she did, they felt bathed in sadness, overwhelmed by memories of how they had made love when they were young. "Was it really worth it?" she said, the skin below her eyes stained with tears.

"God sent me a vision. To spurn it would have been blasphemy."

"You and I will never understand each other." She rolled over, showing him her back.

The children began to approach him. They had grown up assuming their father existed solely in their mother's imagination. Once they had become used to the idea of having a father, his reappearance became a gift. Radu lost his shyness and chatted about his soccer exploits, Irina asked him in a hushed voice about Bucovina. His relations with Ion were more troubled. The boy's friends had told him about Gherla. He seemed to be stifled by his awareness of his father's suffering. Caught between broaching the subject and apparently feeling humiliated by it, he bowed his head.

In 1965, when the young liberalizer Ceauşescu became Romania's leader, they received permission to return to Bucharest. Their new apartment was in a decaying block farther off the Metro line than the apartment where they had lived after the war. The children, though older than most students, were allowed to study. They spoke of the daring books they were reading: books that until recently had been banned. "Be careful," Alina told them. "Don't take any chances. Look at what happened to your father."

Lucian prayed to God to give him patience.

He stood at the gas station staring at a truck. The train had disappeared around a bend. As always now, he was escorted by the past. He felt himself retreating from life with backward steps, his blood bearing him towards his youth. Most days the past overtook his present, plans for activity foundering in formless musings. This morning he had pushed himself to fill his pack, walk to the station and buy a first-class ticket. Now, having reached his destination, he realized that though the village in the valley had become almost unrecognizable — the post-war apartment blocks crumbling, pizza restaurants and internet cafés on the main square, few peasants in wagons and many big trucks — the distance to the mountains was far greater than he remembered.

"You want to go to the mill, sir?" the truck driver said. "I'll take you." As the road climbed and turned to dirt, the driver shifted down through the gears. A red decal pasted to the windshield absorbed the hot sunlight. "The Norwegian flag," the driver explained. "A Norwegian logging company bought the mill last year."

Lucian watched the trucks rolling downhill like barges on wheels, carrying logs to the railway line. *Munți sau mare*: his dispute with Alina had been pointless. The mountains were his sea. He wished it were not too late to tell her that.

"Here we are, sir," the driver said, parking outside the gates.

Lucian climbed out of the truck. Had the mill been rebuilt during the Ceaușescu years, or more recently by these Norwegians? He watched the gates swing open, disgorging a log-heavy truck. An intercom system blared Western music. The guard at the gate swigged a soft drink. He felt springy shavings beneath his feet as he observed the concrete yard. Is this what I fought for? Or is this what I fought to destroy? In his mind he heard a man in Communist garb calling out to God.

"Are you all right, sir?" the driver asked. "You got somewhere to go?"

Lucian stared at the forest. Beyond the beeches and ash dwindling to patchy coniferous bush, alpine meadows glimmered on the edge of the sky. "Yes," he said, setting out towards a path rising between the trees.

A GRAVE IN THE AIR

Ein Mann wohnt im Haus und spielt mit den Schlangen
    der schreibt
der schreibt wenn es dunkelt nach Deutschland
    dein goldenes Haar Margarete
Dein aschenes Haar Sulamith wir schaufeln ein Grab
    in den Lüften da liegt man nicht eng

(A man lives in the house and plays with the snakes
    he writes
he writes when it is dark to Deutschland
    Your golden hair Margarete
Your ashen hair Sulamith we're shovelling a grave
    in the air where rest is uncrowded)
            — Paul Celan, "Todesfuge" ("Death Fuge")

"On that open space, raised a full eight feet upright, stiff and
bare to the waist, the man on the stake remained alone. From a
distance it could only be guessed that the stake to which his legs
had been bound at the ankles passed right through his body. So
that the people saw him as a statue, high up in the air on the very
edge of the staging, high above the river . . .
"Turks, Turks . . . " moaned the man on the stake, "Turks on the
bridge . . . may you die like dogs . . . like dogs."
            — Ivo Andrić, *The Bridge on the Drina*

Darryl walked into the Worldhaus TV building anxious to forget. Rick's message, a fax handed to him this afternoon while he had been easing a box onto a skid, stuttered through his mind. *The case is coming to trial . . . next year in London . . . the people who printed the story saying the Serb atrocities in Bosnia didn't happen . . . a test case . . . your participation . . .* He had read the message so many times that his fingers had left smear-marks on the paper. For the rest of the day he had felt short of breath. And then there had been the panicked reaction of that Slovenian girl . . . so-called Slovenian girl.

He had come here for peace, not to see his past barrel towards him from all sides, urging him to plunge back into everything he had decided to get away from. He had tried phoning Rick this afternoon; but Rick was on a plane to Sierra Leone. Once he had failed to get in touch, Darryl felt his mood change. He lost interest in phoning friends elsewhere. The emotions that had been writhing towards the surface turned on their ends like snakes and buried themselves inside him. There was no one in Weimar with whom he could have the kind of conversation, in English, that he needed to have right now. Walking into the Worldhaus building, he felt furtive and tense, eager for any kind of indulgence, but reluctant to talk.

The equipment was set up, Paul and his band were in the dressing room. Darryl was free until the end of the show. The floodlights in the rafters, vaulted three storeys' height above the hardwood dance floor, came on one after another in a military-perfect test pattern whose solemnity punched holes in the din of low-volume hip hop music. Behind the narrow bar, three attendants were ignoring the crowd while they took a break from serving drinks to chat and rinse out glasses.

"*DDR-Mentalität*," Darryl heard a Pole grumble. "They think this is still East Germany. They think people will accept standing in line-ups . . . !"

Had he not been in such a hurry to get out of Toronto, he would have realized that Weimar in 1999 was not the best place to escape from history. Dates were piling up like rubble from demolished monuments: the tenth anniversary of the fall of the Berlin Wall, the 250th anniversary of the birth of Johann Wolfgang von Goethe, the last summer of the millennium. In a spree footed by the Eurocrats of Brussels, decorated booths on every venerable street corner commemorated the cultural titans. Darryl, whose busy career had allowed him little time to appreciate such pleasures, had resolved when he arrived here to use his off-hours to renew his acquaintance with the finer things in life. But it was not working out that way.

Part of the problem was that his job consisted of lifting and carrying. After an afternoon of moving boxes of musical equipment or setting up stage props and decor, he went back to his room and fell asleep. Beyond this practical barrier lay the double-headed nature of Weimar. "Buchenwald lies just down the road from Weimar . . . " Which German writer had written that? Darryl remembered reading it — perhaps even in German. He had toiled to learn German in the late 1980s and early 1990s, while covering the fall of the Berlin Wall and the reunification movement, just as his years in Central America in the early 1980s had driven him to master Spanish. He was proud of having devoted more time than most journalists to learning the languages of the people whose tragedies he was reporting. He traced the habit back to Canadian bilingualism. Fresh out of J-school, he had been told to brush up his French to cover the Quebec National Assembly. The notion had stuck, instilling in him the belief that a reporter who didn't know a country's language was hamstrung. He had even mustered a passable Serbo-Croatian — though, of course, he had not been able to call it that — by the time he left Bosnia.

Bosnia lay just down the road from Buchenwald... The concentration camp stood over the hill from Weimar, accessible from the Goetheplatz by way of a tram that clattered up through the dense beech trees. Rick, who never missed a detail, had underlined the point. *There will be two genocide trials in London next year... the British historian who denies the Holocaust... since you're sitting below Buchenwald right now let me put it this way... Buchenwald and Bosnia will both be on trial. Neither should have to be proved at this stage... a chance to ensure two crimes aren't forgotten... your participation...*

All Darryl could imagine participating in at the moment was music and dancing. In spite of Rick's fax, he had managed to doze off for a couple of hours before Paul and his band had arrived. Now the night air sharpened his senses. Frustrated by the line-up at the bar, he threaded between the language students from the university's summer academy. He had met many of them at earlier events. There were eastern Germans studying French and Italian, and foreigners studying German. The foreigners came from dozens of countries, though most were young Eastern Europeans, spare and determined in their bluejeans or baggy shorts, the men crewcut, the women wearing their long hair pulled back in loose ponytails from faces scrubbed clean of makeup. Darryl waved to acquaintances and kept moving forward. He saw Magdalena, the lanky Colombian woman he had met a few days earlier at a play in a converted gasworks where he had been arranging the set. She nodded at him as she waited to order her drink, her nod falling short of an invitation.

The hip hop tape was fading. As he approached the speakers, Paul led his band out of the dressing room. The stage was not elevated, and the musicians passed almost unnoticed into the crowd.

He half-expected to see the Slovenian girl step out behind them. He both did and did not want to meet her again. How often in his life had someone responded to him by rushing away with a piercing-eyed, droop-faced expression of terror? In the old days — in Bosnia, of course, but also in El Salvador, Guatemala, Colombia, Croatia and Lebanon — he used to wonder how the men in the death squads and ethnic-cleansing gangs felt staring into the faces of the people they were going to kill. He had imagined the dread reflected in their victims' eyes becoming addictive, like a hit from a euphoria-inducing drug. Yet having struck terror into a young woman he had not much liked, he felt soiled and misunderstood.

"*Von Sankt Petersburg . . . !*" the Worldhaus manager shouted, cupping the microphone. The band's name was lost in the roar. As Paul strolled towards the microphone, backed by his four Russian musicians, Darryl pushed forward. The crowd squeezed into free-flowing rows. Darryl ended up in the second row. Utta, who was managing the band's German tour, stood a few paces in front of him, a video camera hoisted onto her shoulder. She focused on Paul's broad-cheekboned southern African face as the screen overhead came to life. Naked, highly magnified nervousness scurried across Paul's cheeks. Utta swivelled the camera, hauling the musicians onto the screen: three large shaven-headed Russians, small rectangular pelts of hair clinging to the scruffs of their necks, and a short, slight one sporting lank locks beneath a beret. They dug into a reservoir of sound and spilled out a mélange that was not jazz, not rock and roll, not thudding conventional world music, not eastern or western or northern or southern. Their sound was a fusion that refused to fuse: an impatient rifling through the global repertoire of musical expression. One moment the drums sounded African, the next moment the horn-player could have been in a Caribbean salsa band, a few bars later the bass player was cranking up hard-rocking all-American rhythm and blues. Paul sang in Russian and spoke to the audience in French. It made Darryl delirious.

As he started to dance he saw the top of his head pop up on the video screen: one smear of shadow among many. Utta's camera was not alone; the young man Darryl had worked with during the set-up, perched on a platform halfway to the ceiling, was also feeding to the screen. The boys at the back, coordinating the two feeds, cut between the high long shots of the crowd and Utta's close-ups of the band. The first glimpse of the top of his head quelled Darryl's energetic bopping as he picked out the pale scallop of his discreet bald patch. Elsewhere his hair remained as thick as it had been when, gelled, blow-dried and wind-tousled, it had hogged the camera's attention as he had spoken over his microphone against the backdrops of the Quebec National Assembly, Lake Managua, downtown

Bogotá with the peak of Monserrate jutting behind, Berlin and the Brandenburg Gate, Sarajevo Airport. His face remained soft, his body trim and limber; only the permanent hollows below his eyes and the wrinkles that sun or wind brought out, conceded that he was forty. He might not look his age, but neither did he look fresh and youthful: more like a student after an all-night debauch. "You're Faust!" Rick, a brainy graduate of the University of Chicago, had said when Darryl told him his age at the bar of the Sarajevo Holiday Inn. "That's your deal with the devil: the more carnage you see, the younger you look."

Darryl had forgotten Rick's remark until he arrived in Weimar, where the profile of Faust's dramatizer Goethe was stencilled on the window of every souvenir shop. The epic was being performed up the street at the National Theatre on the square. He had passed over the opportunity to attend *Faust* in favour of a night of dancing. It was his new passion, his substitute for other passions too long stifled. Bending his body to the music, he felt liberated and self-mocking. *Your participation . . .* Other men who had been at the scenes of massacres were found drunk in parks, whimpering in hospitals, panting for the needle. Darryl, having travelled from Bosnia to Buchenwald via workout-obsessed Toronto, could only dance. He felt relieved to have found a way to drive out his demons. He coiled and spun and hopped; he drove his body before a thumping beat, letting his limbs float when the music turned mellow. Bald patch or no, he could bop with the best of them. Tomorrow morning he would have stiffer muscles than the young people around him, but tonight he could forget his age. He could forget the terror he carried inside him and had seen reflected in that Slovenian girl's face. He watched his shy friend Paul, transformed by his music, stripping off his vest. Wearing a tattered rag of a shirt yanked open to reveal his sweating black chest, Paul closed his eyes and howled into the microphone in Russian.

Darryl spun around in time to see Magdalena finish her drink and put down the glass on the counter. This time their eyes met with a spark of a smile. She threaded her way towards the front of the room until she was dancing at his side. "*Mucho gusto*," he mouthed over the din as he touched her shoulder.

Their first conversation, at the converted gasworks, had been in Spanish. She had laughed at his Bogotá vocabulary: his use of *chévere* and *vaina*. "When were you in Colombia?"

"During the period when M-19 laid down its arms to take part in elections."

Magdalena had been silent so long that Darryl had feared he had offended her. "How sad," she said, "that I come from a country where time is measured in guerrilla wars." She had left Bogotá to avoid the latest binge of violence, qualifying for a German student visa by writing a proposal for a doctoral thesis in engineering. She was working on developing silage as a source of energy: coaxing heat from dead matter. Her German having proved unequal to the demands of her first year of graduate study, she had come to Weimar for a summer language course. She had a boyfriend or husband — she called him *mi novio* in Spanish and *mein Mann* in German — who had gone away for a few months in circumstances that she did not explain.

On the dance floor her spare bluejeaned hips, weighing into him each time they twisted towards each other, depended from a waist that looked suppler as the Worldhaus building grew hotter. The spot where they were dancing turned into one of those inexplicable alleys that opens up in any crush of humanity, causing everyone moving between the back and the front of the room to try to push between them. The first few times this happened, Darryl and Magdalena sidled apart, keeping time with the music as they let the intruder pass. They began to roll their eyes when people squeezed between them. An hour into the show, as another hunched figure tried to pry them apart, Darryl slid his arm around Magdalena's shoulders, forcing the interloper to the outside. Magdalena peeped at him around the spray of her curly shoulder-length hair. Her light brown cheeks gleamed with sweat. He had never seen such a wide smile on such a narrow face, such aquiline features sprouting such full cheeks. In that instant the music veered from New Orleans jazz to coastal Colombian cumbia. Magdalena's body turned liquid. She shimmered to the cumbia the way only someone who had grown up with the music could. The next time a passer-through tried to elbow between them, she flung her arm around Darryl's waist. He buried his face in her scented hair, trying to pretend that no other time or place existed.

That afternoon the band had stopped at Darryl's apartment.

He had rented a room for the summer in a four-storey, two-hundred-year-old house overlooking Park an der Ilm, where Goethe had reclined under the gingko trees, eyed the milk-maids and scribbled his solemn verse. Each corridor branching off the house's enormous central staircase had been partitioned into a separate flat. The architecture might reach back into the eighteenth century, but the organization of the apartments was unadulterated East German Communist. Each flat was a long wooden corridor flanked by bedrooms. A ledge at the end of the hall remained decked with trays full of nails, screws, bits of broken hinges: the misshapen pieces of metal that people hoarded in societies where spare parts were scarce. Darryl's room had a twelve-foot ceiling, hardwood floors that creaked like old violins and two windows looking out over Park an der Ilm. One window had been almost entirely overgrown by a gnarled jade plant settled in a cauldron-sized pot. A discarded grey 1980s East German Robotron computer, almost as big as a steamer trunk, prevented the pot from keeling over.

The room had no television, and neither did any other room in the apartment. After a lifetime's addiction to the news, Darryl had shut himself off. He had even stopped buying newspapers. His mood pitched between drowsy complacency and outbreaks of information-hunger striped with lashings of guilt. What was happening in Kosovo, Congo, Sierra Leone? In all the places whose stories he had abandoned in midstream by leaving Toronto? Like a recidivist smoker, he stole furtive fixes late at night. Lying on his back in bed, he spun the dial of his Walkman.

Most nights all that was distinguishable through the static was the soporifically cautious tones of Mitteldeutscher Rundfunk broadcasting debates about Sunday shopping in the Leipzig train station or probing microscopic ideological fractures in the Sachsen or Thüringen wings of the Social Democratic Party. Once, as he was drifting off to sleep, the precise diction of the BBC spilled into his ears, sluicing him awake with more facts than he could assimilate. After that, feeling unequal to information, he tried to make good on his resolution to sample the pleasures of culture by reading.

Between the two windows stood an enormous bookcase crammed with books published before the fall of the Berlin Wall. Illustrated introductions to the socialist world written for schoolchildren were packed in next to East German novels published in Leipzig in the 1970s. The novels dealt with young men losing their illusions through experience: usually decadent yet chaste experiences with misguided young women. The novels ended with the young men recognizing that egotism could not compete with the mature pleasure of a full consciousness of the world's problems. They married working-class heroines and braced themselves for a life of class struggle. The protagonists' passion for awareness touched Darryl, reminding him of the ideals that had propelled him into a career in journalism; of all the vestigial traits of East German culture, this desire to know the truth felt the most obsolete.

Darryl was usually alone in the apartment. Nikolai, the tall young Ukrainian economist renting the room next to his, stayed out late; the graduate students who lived in the other four rooms had gone to Berlin for the summer. When Darryl asked Nikolai how he would feel about having Paul's band take over the spare rooms for a few hours, Nikolai said: *"Das wäre sehr kool."*

Darryl had met Paul before, in Havana, where Paul's first, rockier, timidly punkish band had played a few early concerts in the months before the socialist world disintegrated. Once Darryl had realized that this must be the same St. Petersburg-based Zairean he remembered from nearly a decade earlier, when St. Petersburg had been Leningrad, he suggested to the Worldhaus manager that the band use his apartment as a base during their evening in Weimar. By the day of the concert he realized that he was awaiting Paul's arrival with an anticipation rooted more in his own loneliness than in any verifiable emotional bond. Why should a musician who toured as frantically as Paul did remember someone he had met once, nearly a decade earlier? When the door opened, Darryl introduced himself with a laborious explanation in French.

"Of course I remember you!" Paul said. They hugged like earthquake survivors who had been separated in the rubble. Ignoring the clutter of people and instruments following Paul into the flat, Darryl led him to the kitchen. Paul wore a scarf around his throat to protect his voice from the cool, damp Thüringen summer. His skin looked tight, fitted more closely to the hard waves of his cheeks and temples; his black curls had frayed, greyed and receded. Darryl offered Paul a seat at the kitchen table and burned his hand lighting the gas stove to heat the stewed vegetables he had prepared earlier. He passed Paul a bottle of cheap red wine.

In the hall the musicians lined up for the bathroom, razors in hand, to shave their heads for the concert.

"I love travelling with these boys." Paul poured the wine. "We've been on the road for three weeks. And you, Darryl, still the traveller! I saw you on television. I was in a hotel room in Switzerland and you were reporting from Bosnia. A report for French-Canadian television that appeared on TV-Cinq. I shouted when I saw you."

"I stopped travelling," Darryl said, seating himself next to Paul at the small, wobbly kitchen table. "I went home."

"But here you are in Germany."

"It didn't work out. I thought I could forget the world, but the world came looking for me."

"But you must tell me!"

Darryl shrugged his shoulders. "I'm doing an ordinary job now. I set up shows for the summer cultural program. I'm trying to learn about art. I want to appreciate something that lasts."

"Your reports will last," Paul said. "Television is eternal. A hundred years from now people interested in the wars you've covered will be able to watch your reports."

"Right. I'll be embalmed on the airwaves."

"You shouldn't be so cynical. You have a privileged talent. When I die, my CDs will be forgotten."

"I could never make music . . . How do you invent sound?"

Utta and Nikolai, who had struck up a conversation in Russian, sat down at the table. Darryl and Paul continued to chat in French, but Darryl could see that Paul's concentration had been broken. "Eat your stewed vegetables," he said. "They're good for your throat."

Utta addressed Paul in Russian. Releasing the grip he had taken on Darryl's arm, Paul responded with a despairing shrug of his shoulders.

An amused smile took shape on Nikolai's face. "They have problems with the band," he explained to Darryl in German. "Women problems."

Utta, who was handling the band's German tour to finance her doctorate in Russian poetry, turned on Nikolai. "These are not women problems," she said, speaking German so that Darryl would understand. "These are men problems. Such problems would not exist if men knew how to behave."

She got to her feet and left the kitchen.

"Oy," Nikolai said. "She's going to get Yury. Now the man will be in trouble." His handsome face gleamed.

Paul leaned forward, cradling his wine. "You see, Darryl, these boys are wonderful musicians, but they are young. They had never left St. Petersburg until we began touring. In St. Petersburg we have a club where we jam for hours. We throw in sounds we've picked up from other groups, noises we've heard on the street — "

"But where does the music *come from*?"

"From inside us." He looked over his shoulder into the corridor. "I've never played with such creative musicians. There's always something new happening. But on the road, unfortunately, they are not very disciplined. They like the attention, they like the late nights. They like the girls."

Utta returned to the kitchen followed by one of the lumbering, shaven-headed youths. Yury was the bass player. His shiny skull and the studs clamped into his earlobes accentuated the peasant stolidity of his face. Five of them sat around the table. Darryl swallowed a surreptitious gulp of wine while Yury picked at the low collar of his white flannel shirt. Utta stared at Yury with suppressed rage, then cast an expectant glance towards Paul. Before Paul could speak, Nikolai began to ramble in loquacious Russian. Darryl, accustomed to Nikolai's astute, steamrolling disquisitions, waited for Utta to lose her patience. But it was Paul who spoke.

Nudging his scarf, Paul delivered a melancholy rebuke. He warned Yury that a man, particularly a foreigner, cannot treat Western women as disposable objects. When you are a guest in a country you must be careful — especially when the women are little more than young girls.

Yury stared at the table, while Paul explained to Darryl in French what he had said. Nodding towards Nikolai, he said: "Your friend has a very strong Ukrainian accent!"

"How old were you when you learned Russian?" Darryl asked Nikolai in German.

"No," Nikolai said. "My family comes from the south of Ukraine, where most people are Russian — Russian is my first language, but Russian with a Ukrainian accent!"

Aware of the murmur of Utta's voice as she relayed the conversation to Paul in Russian, Darryl said: "And now you are living in an independent Ukraine."

"It doesn't matter where one lives," Nikolai said. "Russia, Ukraine, Belarus, Poland — it's all Eastern Europe."

Yury, who had been keeping his domed head down, looked up. Darryl realized that he understood more German than he was letting on. He made a long, vehement speech in Russian. Utta and Paul looked stern, but Nikolai laughed. "Ha! My friend here does not think that history can be so easily forgotten. But history is in the past."

"How did you get a visa to come to Germany?" Utta asked, as Darryl marvelled at Nikolai's charisma: at how his size, his good looks and articulateness rerouted conversation from any topic, no matter how pressing, towards him and his concerns.

"In the early 1990s the German government had a special visa program," Nikolai said. "For Jews."

"You're Jewish?" Utta said. "And you want to go back to Ukraine? But during the Second World War the Ukrainians — "

"So did the Germans," Nikolai said. "You will recall that the Germans were much worse. But today I am happy in the shadow of Buchenwald. I am aware of this history, but it does not reflect my experience. I must lead my own life, based on what I have lived."

As Nikolai repeated his comments in Russian for the benefit of Yury and Paul, high heels sounded in the corridor. The girl pushed into the kitchen, settling her large hand on Yury's bent shoulder. As Darryl tried to count her rings, she said: "*Warum sprichst du mit dieser Leute? Das ist sehr langweilig für mich. Du magst mich nicht?*" The girl's haughty gaze ranged over the table. Though she spoke with an audible Slavic accent, she sounded as though she had been in Germany for months.

Darryl felt himself staring at her, and realized that the others were, too. The girl lapped it up, hovering above them like an angel: the only person in the room who wasn't seated. She was a tall, broad-shouldered young woman with a soft, conventionally pretty face, mouse-coloured eyebrows and long unkempt centre-parted brown hair. She wore flared slacks and enormous black shoes with wedge heels. "I'm so out of it," she announced in loud, slightly slurry German. "I didn't go to bed until five a.m. I haven't had more than four hours' sleep any night this week!"

Utta, twisted around in her chair to stare at the girl, looked ready to scratch her. To relieve the pressure, Darryl asked: "Is that how long you've been travelling with the band?"

"We met at the concert in Göttingen. I was so bored in Göttingen!"

Paul asked Yury the girl's age. She said she was seventeen, then gave vent to a mewing laugh that broke her large, womanly body into a rubbery crescent.

"Where are you from?" Nikolai asked in German. "What language do you speak together?"

"We just talk," the girl said, as Yury's face took on a fixed stillness. "We understand each other. Yury understands a little German and I can read the Russian alphabet. I'm from Slovenia. My papa sent me to Göttingen for the summer to improve my German. Papa owns the best construction company in Ljubljana!"

In the back of Darryl's mind, a shadow fell. How did this girl know the Cyrillic alphabet? Hadn't Slovenia stopped teaching that alphabet — which wasn't really the Russian alphabet, but the Serbian modification of it — in 1991 or 1992, when the republic was breaking away from Yugoslavia? How old would she have been then? Ten? She didn't seem like the sort of girl to remain proficient in a second alphabet she had been taught briefly at the beginning of primary school. "You learned the Russian alphabet at school in Ljubljana?" he asked.

No one was listening. Paul looked uncomfortable and Utta ever more hostile. Nikolai's queries about life in Ljubljana had prompted the girl to embark on a tour of the city's discos. "The discos in Göttingen aren't nearly as good."

Darryl tried to ask his question again, but felt too dispirited to assert himself the way he used to in media scrums.

"You Slovenes try to pretend you were never part of Eastern Europe," Nikolai said. "You think you're so rich and Westernized it must have been a mistake — "

The girl looked bored. "I don't talk about politics. I just want to have a good time."

"Bah!" For once Nikolai was at a loss for words.

Utta, peering from beneath her level bangs, said: "Do you have a boyfriend in Ljubljana?"

She dropped a cutting glance in the direction of Yury, who continued to contemplate the middle of the table. His freshly shaven skull gleaming, he reached out and emptied the last of Darryl's bottle into a convenient coffee mug.

"*Ja,*" the girl said, her body writhing in confessional agony. "I have a boyfriend. But he's boring. *Er ist keine Sexmaschine.*"

Nikolai whooped. "And Yury is a sex-machine? Yury — !" Nikolai switched into Russian, clapping Yury on the shoulder.

"You have had many boyfriends," Utta said.

"Didn't you go to discos when you were seventeen? Didn't you have boyfriends?"

"When I was seventeen," Utta said, scowling at the girl, "I lived in East Germany."

Except, Darryl thought, filtering the conversation into English in his mind, Utta hadn't said: "I lived in East Germany"; she had said: "*Das war die DDR-Zeit.* It was the East German period." A different epoch, a different history, had constrained the possibilities of her youth.

"My God," Utta said, "I'm only eleven years older than her and it's as if we were born a hundred years apart."

She pushed past the girl and left the kitchen. No one went after her.

Paul looked at Darryl with an anxious expression. Darryl felt that they were both very old: a dozen years older than Utta, nearly a quarter-century older than the girl. "I must tell her to leave," Paul murmured in French. "She must go back to her German classes. If she stays, she will destroy us. I didn't realize she was so young. Her father could accuse us of kidnapping her."

He pulled out Utta's chair and motioned to the girl to sit down. She collapsed in a long-limbed crumple; her arms trailed over the table, her hair fell across her cheeks. Bending forward, Paul spoke to her in Russian in a fatherly tone of voice. The girl looked blank. Her Russian did not appear to extend beyond a knowledge of the alphabet. "Help me, Darryl," Paul said in French. "Tell her she can't stay."

The girl glanced in Darryl's direction. Her mouth twisted. "You have to understand," Darryl said in German. "You can't — I'm sorry, what's your name?"

"Latifa."

Darryl swallowed his next sentence. He saw Paul glancing at him. Nikolai leaned closer, while Yury examined the nicotine-stained lids of his fingernails. His voice nearly shaking, he asked: "What's your last name, Latifa?"

"Hasanović, Latifa Hasanović."

Darryl felt his fingertips pressing into the chipped paint of the table. Latifa grew still. He saw a tension tightening her skin, banishing the floppy girlishness from her big body. The longer he remained silent, the more agitated Latifa became. Her fingers twisted, pulling higher in a way that drew her elbows across the table like bent pendulums. Almost before the words were out, Darryl wished he could smother his newshound's automatic reaction: "That's not a Slovenian name, it's a Bosnian name. You're a Bosnian Muslim."

"No." Latifa's eyes looked darker and darker. Everyone else in the room vanished. Darryl stared into Latifa's face. Her features grew pale and heavy. Her chin began to tremble. She pushed at the table in front of her.

Darryl grabbed her arm. "You're related to Mullah Hasanović. You must be!"

She pulled away from him, her chair tipping back against the fridge. "What do I care? I never met him! He's dead! They're all dead!"

"I knew the Mullah's son!"

"Let go! You're hurting me!"

Darryl released her arm, shocked by the force of his own grip. Latifa fell back against the fridge, the chair clattering over between her legs. She kicked herself upright. "I'm Slovenian! Don't you understand? I'm never going to be Bosnian again!"

Before Darryl could reply, she rushed down the hall. Yury, roused from his paralysis, called out in Russian. The loud beat of Latifa's clogs sounded on the bare hardwood; the front door slammed behind her.

Yury was on his feet, staring at Darryl, who was struggling to control his panting breath.

"She's related to somebody you knew in Bosnia?" Paul asked. "A mullah who was killed in the war?"

"Yes. But not this Bosnian war — the last one. Mullah Hasanović died in 1943."

You choose to remember, Darryl thought, or you choose to forget. Life had required him to compress each country into a few polished anecdotes. He displayed these ancedotes, nugget-like, at parties, when strangers asked him about life as a foreign correspondent. Refining his representative tale of each time and place, he forgot the rest, in the way that people recalled every detail of their vacation photographs but remembered nothing else about the places they had visited.

Then there were the events that he never mentioned but could not forget, such as his friendship with the Hasanović family.

He had interviewed them in his third-floor room in the Sarajevo Holiday Inn. A rangy fifty-two-year-old man wearing a zippered track-suit jacket over grey slacks and a long-sleeved dress shirt, his much younger wife garbed in the *dimije* of the Muslim countryside, her head cloaked in a scarf though her face remained unveiled, and two silent adolescent boys who watched television at low volume. Three older children, two married girls and a boy, had been scattered by the war. Having dismissed his interpreter, Darryl had struggled to speak to Mohamed and Emina in the language that no longer had a name: the language that under Marshal Tito had been Serbo-Croatian. Now the Croats, introducing new vocabulary in the hope of making themselves incomprehensible to Serbs, used a language called Croatian, while the Serbs, retreating into the Cyrillic alphabet, spoke and wrote Serbian. In Montenegro and Bosnia people rejected all three designations, referring to "this language that we speak." The small blue book with whose aid he had half-learned the language claimed to be providing instruction in "Bosnian." He sweated to make himself understood. He disliked interviewing in the hideous yellow-walled Holiday Inn. The enormous open foyer tapering upwards several floors above the reception desk made him feel as though his room were perched inside the spire of a cathedral: a dim, sepulchral box poised in space.

The interview began to flow only after Darryl gave up on his fractured "Bosnian" and switched to German. Mohamed Hasanović had worked as a mason in Austria for twelve years. Speaking German was a common attainment among rural Bosnian men, though less common in the mining region around Srebrenica where fewer men than elsewhere had to leave the country to find work. Mohamed came not from Srebrenica itself, but from a nearby village. Here work was less plentiful and Mohamed's brothers had all gone to Austria or Germany as soon as Tito had opened the borders. They sent back money, saved money. His oldest, most entrepreneurial brother had invested his Deutschmarks earned on German construction sites in a trailer truck. He had hauled goods from Sarajevo to Zagreb to Ljubljana to Munich or Milan. After a few years he had bought two more trucks, and turned over the driving to younger men while he managed his business from an office in Sarajevo. "His youngest daughter was born in Sarajevo. She has never known her father as anything but a prosperous man from the city."

"Are these older brothers or younger brothers?" Darryl asked, trying to establish a chronology.

"All older. I was the last."

"The last?" The phrasing sounded odd, though it might be Mohamed's German.

"My parents' last child. I was born three months after my father was killed."

"When was that?"

"1943."

"He was killed by the Germans?"

"No, by the Chetniks."

"You mean the Serbs?" Darryl paused. His knowledge of the history was still shaky at this point. He did not realize that many of the Yugoslavs who died during the Second World War had been killed not by the occupying army of Nazi Germany but by other Yugoslavs. After recording Mohamed Hasanović's story Darryl began to study this history; he came to see the ethnic cleansing he had reported on three years earlier in a historical context that rendered him uncomfortable with recent coverage of the war, including his own.

Mullah Hasanović, as he was addressed by Muslims in the villages, had begun his adult life as a wandering *hodža*, or holy man. He had received a strict training in Sarajevo after the First World War: studying the Koran, learning to read Arabic and Persian, and writing the unnameable language not only in the modified Cyrillic that was Bosnia's first alphabet but also in the Croats' Latin letters and the streaming curlicues of classical Arabic. He regarded the beggars in Sarajevo's streets as "God's people," and was careful to hand them the leftover Austrian kronen bills, the denominations overprinted to accommodate hyperinflation, that served as the currency of the newly declared Kingdom of Serbs, Croats and Slovenes. He had completed his training with a peripatetic dervish who had instructed him in numerology. Having grown up in eastern Bosnia, Mullah Hasanović longed to alleviate the spiritual blight afflicting Muslims in the villages. Nomadic *hodžas* offered the only religious sustenance most villagers would ever know; their prayers, and instructions to swallow pieces of paper on which verses from the Koran had been written, provided them with their only medical attention. Post-First World War land reforms had reduced many Muslim families to landless poverty.

Mullah Hasanović renounced the pleasures of Sarajevo, with its magnificent library where he had perfected his literary Persian, and its tasty *cevapćići*, for the remote mountain world where he was needed.

"When I first went to work in Austria," Mohamed said, "my father came to me in dreams to reproach me for abandoning eastern Bosnia. I argued with him, crying out in my sleep that I was more use to my family sending money home from Salzburg than sitting around drunk in the village. But he wore me out. He floated before my eyes. He is the reason I went back."

The boys stared at the television, betraying no interest in their father's earnest German. Emina, Mohamed's bright-eyed wife, followed the conversation with her head bowed. Did she understand German, or was she so familiar with this story that she recognized it even in a foreign language?

Darryl waited for the tram to pass. It seemed barely credible that the tram, closed down by the first Serb mortar attacks, was running again. "My oldest brother, the one with the trucking business — he moved to Ljubljana when the war broke out. He used to have a photograph of our father." Their father had been a tall man, even taller than Mohamed himself. He wore embroidered waistcoats, open jackets, zouave trousers bunched at the knee. Unlike city-dwelling Muslims in their heel-less shoes with upturned toes, Mullah Hasanović wore a pair of leather boots he had bought in the market in Sarajevo. Shod in his boots he could hike thirty kilometres a day through the oblong, upended-looking, cloud-streaked bright green Bosnian mountains slashed by the plunging ravines of the river valleys. In the villages he entered, the mosques were in ruins, or there were no mosques at all. Many of the villages contained as many

Serbs as Muslims, and sometimes he would consent also to visit ailing Serbs, just as, in one village along the ferocious Drina River that formed the border between Bosnia and Serbia, Serb peasants had collected money to assist their Muslim neighbours in repairing the mosque's caved-in roof. Parents would round up the local boys for instruction in Arabic script and reading from the Koran. Mullah Hasanović would teach the boys, then question their parents to ensure that during his last visit the barber — another itinerant profession — had properly circumcised their newborn sons. He would learn which girls had eloped, and whether they had gone to good homes. He cautioned families where husbands beat their new brides excessively, or where their mothers-in-law worked them like slaves. When his duties were complete, Mullah Hasanović would eat with the Muslim men, and sometimes the Serbian men as well, laugh at their jokes, tolerate their drinking and dispense advice. "He was a very sociable man," Mohamed said.

"He liked women too much," Emina said in the unnameable language. "That's what your mother said."

Mohamed glanced at his wife, then at Darryl. Seeing that Darryl had understood, he said to his wife in their own language, very slowly: "My mother was aged when you met her. Her memory was no longer good."

Emina looked in the direction of the boys and bit her lip.

"After a few years of this life," Mohamed said in German, "my father settled in the village where I was born. He took a young wife — I have followed in his footsteps by marrying a woman younger than I." Emina looked up as though breathless. "But my father did not forget his duties to the villagers."

He had his own faithful to care for now, his own small mosque whose delicate white minaret jabbed up through the beech trees on a low hillside. His years of walking had made him boney and lean-ribbed and angular beneath the beard that showed a speckling of grey. He read the Koran deep into the evening by the light of paired guttering candles until his eyes grew too sore to focus on the squiggly script. He sipped plum brandy on the sly to dull the pain of throbbing teeth, which wandering barbers pulled for him when the aching became unendurable. Through books obtained by mail order, he renewed his youthful acquaintance with classical Persian literature. The sight of the modified Arabic script of Persian returned him to his student days reading in the stately library in Sarajevo. The respect in which he was held in the village increased as each of his children proved to be a son. Women from far around came to ask his counsel on family decisions. He would write down the names of all involved, calculate the numerological value of the Cyrillic letters, divide by the secret quotient, dispense advice and accept a small payment for his services. He never asked exorbitant fees. His sons ensured him a prosperous old age, unlike fathers who brought up daughters destined to elope at seventeen and lend their labour to other men's homes.

In his position other *hodža*s might have indulged their authority, and swaggered around the village enjoining unyielding religious observance. But Mullah Hasanović, both introverted and spiritually restless, kept to himself. Two or three times a year restiveness of spirit translated into restiveness of limb and he would set off on the road, visiting the villages where people remembered him as having been for years their only source of knowledge. His boots, repaired many times by a cobbler in Srebrenica, no longer carried him thirty kilometres a day. He accepted more rides in ox-drawn carts, took greater care not to be caught outside after dark and rarely travelled in the winter. Once, Mullah Hasanović fell ill with pneumonia. It happened in Višegrad, near the bridge across the Drina River built by Mehmet Pasha, the 16th-century Serbian boy who, after converting to Islam, had risen to become the wisest, most powerful minister of Suleiman the Magnificent, going down in history as a hero to both Muslims and Serbs. The bridge's indomitable arches, its impressive height — made less evident by its great, flattened length — swirled in Mullah Hasanović's delirious dreams. He was brought home weeks later in the back of a wagon, and spent the next summer convalescing while his strong young sons cared for the cattle and the mosque. But within a year he was on the road again, his months on his back having filled him with fresh learning to share. "His will was unstoppable," Mohamed said.

Emina's dark irises swelled. Darryl realized that a late marriage to a much younger woman might not be all that Mohamed Hasanović and his father shared. What happened when a man spent twelve years away from his wife? He imagined Mohammed passing his evenings in Salzburg, while his wife lived under the scrutiny of pious neighbours who had known her all her life.

Whatever the source of the urges that sent Mullah Hasanović marching into the hills, he refused to allow the Second World War to diminish them. Bosnia was annexed by the Croatian fascist regime whose brutality stunned even its Nazi masters. At Jasenovac, just over the border from Bosnia, the Croats established the third-largest concentration camp of the Second World War, where they murdered Jews, gypsies, Muslims, but above all Serbs, transformed by the Ustasha classification system into "Greek-Easterns." Yet the Ustasha stormtroopers were little in evidence in Mullah Hasanović's village. In 1941 the Ustasha staged a pogrom in Srebrenica, murdering the town's Jewish population. Some Muslim men joined the Ustasha and participated in the massacre. Mullah Hasanović did not condemn their actions. Muslims were joining all sides in this war; it was the only way to survive. There were Muslims fighting for fascist Croatia, special Muslim units among Tito's Communist Partisans, and even Muslims marching in the ranks of Colonel Mihailović's long-bearded royalist Chetniks, whose leaders dreamed of a Greater Serbia. Only the latter made Mullah Hasanović nervous, but even among the Chetniks he had friends. A Serb family that had brought him food during his convalescence in Višegrad had contributed two sons to the ranks of Mihailović's non-commissioned officers, and these boys had persuaded some of the Muslim boys he had tutored to join them. Mullah Hasanović preferred not to take sides. He repeated to his community the instructions of Fehim Spaho, the *Reis ul-ulema*, or Muslim religious leader of Bosnia, to scorn mixed marriages and non-Muslim names for children. As long as these rules were adhered to, he counselled his wife, sons and neighbours, history would rush past them like the wind. They would reap the harvest they merited.

Battles raged all over eastern Bosnia. Between the battles came long periods of calm. German troops arrived to support their Ustasha allies, Tito's partisans passed through on three occasions, Mihailović's troops drove towards the Drina from inside Serbia. But, deprived of its young men and its mainly imported foodstuffs, the village felt austere, impoverished and unbearably quiet. By the end of September, 1943, Mullah Hasanović was bored. His legs ached for the hills. He made a trip into Srebrenica to have his boots repaired. Then, in spite of the moodiness of his three sons, aged fifteen, thirteen and eight, and shrugging off the misgivings of his six-months'-pregnant wife, he set out to see the villagers he knew were waiting for him.

"I know almost nothing of my father's final days," Mohamed said. Mullah Hasanović hiked south over the hills towards Višegrad. He must have stayed in villages along the way, visited old friends, instructed boys in writing Arabic and reading the Koran. He would have slept in the homes of families he had visited many times before. It is hard to believe that he did not hear rumours of how Colonel Mihailović's royalists, freshly supplied with weapons and ammunition by Winston Churchill, had turned their drive against the Nazis and the Ustasha into a campaign of slaughter against Muslims on both sides of the Drina. "I think perhaps he knew his life would end soon anyway and he wanted to see the Drina one more time," Mohamed said. Mullah Hasanović liked to speak of the exhilaration that came over him as he approached the river and saw the mountains surge free of their green garb of pastures and beech woods to press against the sky in flinty ridges. It was a vision that brought him closer to Allah.

He must have reached Višegrad around October 2. On October 5 Mihailović's Chetniks, accompanied by British and American advisers, attacked the city. A relative claimed that when the attack began Mullah Hasanović was in the home of the Serbian family who had brought him food during his illness. The history books reported that the attack was launched at dawn. No one knew what the Mullah was doing in a Serbian family's home so early in the morning.

The Germans and Croats fled the Chetnik attack, rushing back into Bosnia across Mehmet Pasha's bridge. Snipers gunned them down as they ran. So many bodies clogged the bridge that ox-drawn carts could no longer pass over them. The Chetniks entered the town and went door to door, dragging Muslims into the centre of the bridge and tossing them over the side into the river below. For two weeks Mihailović's men killed not only military-age youths, but also old Muslim women and young children. The young women were locked up and raped. The young men who were able to escape fled to join the Ustasha or the Partisans. The British and American advisers observed the slaughter, realizing only gradually that the Chetniks' idea of the enemy was not the same as theirs.

Mullah Hasanović's Višegrad relative maintained that the Mullah had asked the Serbian family to hide him. But, afraid of reprisals if he were discovered, they refused. It is possible the Mullah did not request this favour from his Serbian friends. It is possible they offered to hide him and it was he who said no out of a fear of endangering their lives. Or perhaps the two families were no longer associating with one another. What is nearly certain is that on the morning of October 9, Chetniks burst into the back room of the Muslim house where Mullah Hasanović was squinting at the Koran. Calling him a Turk and an Ustasha, they hustled him through the streets into the centre of Mehmet Pasha's bridge. The cold air was a shock. He saw snow on the hillsides above him, the gashes where the indomitable white bridge had been struck by artillery fire, a twisted body, frosted rinds of dung, a dog slurping at a splash of fresh blood, a pallid-looking man in a foreign officer's uniform patrolling with a dull stare.

Hands tightened on his arms. "One-two-three and we heave him over the side," a soldier said close his ear.

A Chetnik officer who had been standing next to the foreigner intervened. "This one's a *hodža*. Slit his throat."

In this way the death of Mullah Hasanović entered a British officer's report on the atrocities committed by Mihailović's Chetniks. In Toronto, Darryl found a reference to the incident in a history of Yugoslavia during the Second World War. A month after the Mullah's death, Winston Churchill broke with Mihailović and began to support Tito, who, he said, was more focused on "killing Germans."

The blade felt colder than the morning air. Practised in what they did, the Chetniks slit Mullah Hasanović's throat from his right ear to his left ear, releasing a collar of warm blood. Cold air flowed into his body through the wound in his neck. There was almost no pain. As his feet left the ground, a Persian mystic's passage on levitation passed through his mind.

"The Drina became his grave," Darryl said. "You said he liked the Drina."

"No," Mohamed said, as the tram clattered past the Holiday Inn. "A Muslim's soul leaves his body the second he dies. They must have waited at least a moment between slitting his throat and throwing him over the side. I think he died on the way down. His soul left his body in space. The air is his grave. When I am in eastern Bosnia, I feel I myself inhaling my father."

As the band's last encore ended Darryl clasped Magdalena's wrist. "I have to load the van. Will you wait for me?"

The glare of the house lights dispersed clinging pairs of dancers. Magdalena blinked. The sheen of sweat on her cheeks dimmed, the strong light raising fine wrinkles around the corners of her eyes. "I don't want to stay here when everyone's leaving." She looked in the direction of the dormant video screen. "I should go to bed. I have to phone my husband tomorrow morning."

Mi marido. It was the first time she had referred to her vanished partner with a word that unambiguously meant "husband."

Darryl searched Magdalena's face for a sign that the word had been intended as a warning. "It's not only the van," he said. He explained his unintentional exposure of Latifa's past. "It just came out. I didn't realize she would react so — "

"Go," Magdalena said. "Load up the van. See if Latifa's there."

He shrugged into his jacket, feeling the cool lining soaking up the sweat from his arms and shoulder blades.

In the dark, cold parking lot behind the building Darryl helped Yury carry a drum-case into the back of the van. The musicians were arranging their luggage and equipment around the edges of the van's floor; in the middle they had unfurled three sleeping bags. They would take turns sleeping, driving and squatting on the tiny fold-down seats.

"Did the girl come back?" Darryl asked, touching Yury's elbow.

This time Yury did not understand German.

"She found another man," Utta said from behind the steering wheel. "Didn't you see her? She was dancing at the back with your Ukrainian friend."

"With Nikolai?" Darryl stepped around the corner of the van until he was looking in the window. "Did you see which way they went?" As Utta shook her head, he said: "I wish I'd realized she was Bosnian."

"If she's Bosnian she shouldn't pretend to be Slovenian. I don't pretend to be western German. A girl like that has a very easy life. She should be made to think harder."

"She has an easy life *now* — "

Utta turned away, conferring with the horn player over a road map. Paul laid his hand on Darryl's shoulder. He had put on his vest and jacket, and wrapped the scarf around his neck.

"It was fabulous," Darryl said. "It was great to talk."

"Who knows when we'll meet again, Darryl. Maybe I'll see you on television?"

Behind Paul's back the shaggy drummer lit a joint. He toked and passed the joint to Yury.

Darryl shook his head. "That's finished. Next time I'll be the one who sees you on television playing your music."

"You're not going to Rwanda? Reports on Bosnia, monuments to Buchenwald . . . Isn't it time for a monument to the people killed in Rwanda?"

"I'll have to leave that to someone else." As gently as he tried to speak the words, Darryl felt a distance setting in between them. He wanted to mention Latifa, but could not think how to bring up her name. The band's failure to react to her disappearance unnerved him.

As he and Paul embraced, Darryl's instinct told him that they would not meet again. He used to think his intuition was infallible, but he had already erred once tonight. It was time to withdraw . . . into what? *Your participation.* Rick's fax cried out for an answer. He thought about what would be required of him if he consented to appear as a witness at the libel trial of the London magazine that had reprinted in English an obscure German journalist's article claiming that the genocide of Muslims in northern Bosnia in 1992 and 1993 was a fabrication of an Islam-loving Western media. A story which, like the nearly concurrent forthcoming trial of a Holocaust-denying British historian on a similar libel charge, tried to obliterate memory. He thought of the days of preparation, the hours of being grilled by caustic English barristers. It made him want to run away. But he had run away. And where had he run to? To Weimar, to the fringes of Buchenwald.

Releasing Paul, he felt that they were already far apart.

"Good luck in Leipzig," he said, as Paul turned away to bed down in the van. "Good luck on the rest of your tour."

Utta turned the van out of the parking lot without waving.

When he returned to the Worldhaus TV building the house lights had gone off, the bar was closed, but Magdalena was standing by the door. He hurried towards her.

"Did you find the girl?" When Darryl shook his head, Magdalena said: "She must be a stupid girl to run away like that." Taking his hand, she led him down the front steps of the Worldhaus building. A few recalcitrant party-goers sat at picnic tables in the dark, sloshing back the evening's last beers. "Come for a walk with me."

The sidewalks were silent. The fissures in the plaster of the unrenovated East Bloc buildings turned to black trickles beneath the murky streetlights. "Thank you for waiting, Magdalena."

"You should be old enough to know you can usually persuade a woman to stay by making her feel needed." A faint wire of bitterness edged her smile.

Their shoulders grazed. The net of their fingers had unravelled, her psychological acuity had thrown him off balance. He felt closer and closer to her. His blood beat softly through his ears.

They walked towards the centre of the city.

"Do you want to see where I live?" Her eyes flung a dare in his direction. She laughed with a tensed protrusion of her jaw that made her boney, light brown face look fascinatingly ugly, then jovial and handsome again. Darryl pulled her towards him. He kissed her to fix her joviality in place. The kiss went on longer than he had expected.

Magdalena lived on the top floor of an anonymous modern student residence block where the front door remained unlocked all night. A light came on as they opened the door. Climbing the stairs, they heard the echo of another pair of feet a couple of flights below them. The thought that they weren't the only ones out this late made them laugh, tumble together and begin kissing again.

When they reached the top floor Magdalena took Darryl's wrist. "I want to show you something."

She led him to a tiny white-tiled kitchen. "Look," she said, opening the window. Darryl leaned out. Beyond the low rooftops the dark mass of the hills was split by a node of lights. It was the Buchenwald monument: a Stalinist memorial to the victims of Nazism. The gargantuan column tossed heroically striding human figures far up into the air. The distance, darkness and piercing glare of the lights rendered the figures invisible. Darryl imagined their rigid forms sailing above the beech trees.

Magdalena pushed her head out the window. They wrapped their arms around each other. "Sometimes I come here when I'm having trouble figuring out how to turn silage into a source of energy. And I wonder if they'll put up a monument to the victims of *La Violencia* if the war in Colombia ever ends. 60,000 dead in Buchenwald. That many people die every couple of years in Colombia. But since we're all the same nationality, it's not genocide. If one race were killing another, the world would stop it."

"Only when it was convenient to stop it. That's what happened in Yugoslavia. The West only stopped the war once the minorities had been killed or driven out." Darryl felt restless. The conversation was dissipating his obsession with Magdalena's skin and hair and eyes. He wondered where Latifa was. He saw Mohamed and Emina and their sons trekking over the hills above Zlvorh and Mullah Hasanović tumbling through space. A twitch of Magdalena's long legs drove these images from his mind. He kissed her cheeks, cool from the night air, and ran his hands in cupped strokes over her hips. "I hope your room isn't too far away."

"Just down the hall."

He followed her into the fluorescent glare of the corridor. The glow of her curls was so beautiful that his breath caught at the thought that he would soon see her hair brushing her naked shoulders.

Magdalena planted a kiss on his mouth as she reached into her bluejeans for her keys. Darryl realized he had taken a step back. "Magdalena, would you mind . . . ? Would it be all right if we went to my room instead?"

She looked stunned with impatient desire. "What's the matter with my room?"

"I want to be with you." He stepped forward and laid his hands on her hips. "But I want — "

"You think we can do this whenever it suits you? I didn't come here to betray my husband, you know. I've only done this once before in eleven years of marriage and it caused a lot of damage."

"I didn't mean . . . " he said, wrenched by her wince. "I'm just worried about Latifa."

"Fine! Go see your little Latifa then." Magdalena drew a shuddering breath. She laid her palm on the doorhandle. "I was willing to take a chance for you, Darryl — "

Her stare made his legs weak. He drew a quick breath, clenching his fists, then walked away.

"After my father was killed," Mohamed said, "my two older brothers ran away and joined the Ustasha. They came back in the night and killed Serbs in villages along the Drina — the same villages where my father had taught Muslim boys and feasted with Serbs while the villagers danced together and sang their *sevdalinkas*. My brothers escaped at the end of the war, when Tito executed Mihailović and the Ustasha leaders. They didn't even go to jail. Everyone knew, of course. Everyone knew which side everyone else had been on. But now we were all living together in peace. It was Brotherhood and Unity, and we all had portraits of Comrade Tito on the wall. The history of the war they printed in the newspapers and showed on television and taught to the children in school spoke only of the heroic struggle of the Communist Partisans against Nazi fascism. No Muslims had been killed by Serbs, no Serbs had been killed by Croats, and only the Nazis had killed Jews. People of my generation were taught this version of history at school. We learned a different version at home. We knew which version was correct: we could smell it in the air of the villages, see it in the missing relatives, the people who distrusted each other, the men who dismantled Second World War weapons, oiled the parts and buried them in crates in their gardens. But outside our homes, no one talked about these things. Not until they started to happen again."

"So it was history coming back?" Darryl said. "Ancient hatreds repeating themselves?"

"No!" Mohamed said. "There are no ancient hatreds, just complicated ways of living together. I was not born hating anyone. What destroyed us wasn't history. It was forty-five years of not being allowed to talk about history. We lost our memory. I speak German — I know the Germans had to face what they did in the war. We never did. We were taught something untrue. People who had committed crimes didn't have to confront what they had done so others felt free to do it again."

Darryl thought about Mohamed's words when he woke up at night to the sound of shelling and sniper fire, when explosions made the hotel reel and bucked his bed in small skids across the carpet. From amid the familiar perils of Sarajevo, he had reported on the ethnic cleansing of Muslims in eastern Bosnia

during 1992 and 1993 without realizing that this had happened
before. The whole time he and Rick had been interviewing
refugees from northern Bosnia on the Croatian border, he had
not known that he was watching history repeat itself. Shorn of
context, his reports seemed nonsensical to him now. In 1993 he
and Rick had attended peace negotiations at Sarajevo Airport,
where he saw the Bosnian Serb General, Ratko Mladić, for
the first time. Mladić's tense, sickly face, bearing the wincing
smile of a man with a perpetual stomach ache, held Darryl's
attention even when others were speaking. Rick whispered to
Darryl that as a child Mladić had hidden in a tree while the
Ustasha killed his mother. Hilde claimed that Mladić's father
had also been killed by the Ustasha, and that his body had never
been found. Later, when Mohamed and Emina and the boys left
Sarajevo in the spring of 1995, and later still, after the massacre
in Srebrenica that summer, he began to see the past hanging in
the air wherever he went.

Srebrenica finished him as a foreign correspondent. He
stayed on in Sarajevo one more year, until the summer of 1996,
in order to be able to visit the scene of the massacre. He had to
quit his job and go freelance to stay put; after late 1995, Bosnia
was no longer headline news. Darryl was ordered to move
on. He could not pry himself away from the ruined city. He
had to see Srebrenica. And part of him remained hopelessly
attached to the naive, madcap desperation of his first two years
in Sarajevo.

The exuberance of those years! In spite of the Serb shells
crashing into every apartment block, flattening every mosque,
cathedral and synagogue, Darryl felt reborn. He was immune
to the lack of electricity, the frigid rooms and sputtering water

supply, the nights robbed of sleep by bombardments that left him light-headed with fatigue in the brooding mountain daylight. Sarajevo's setting reminded him of Bogotá, Colombia — but a Bogotá sparser in population and denser in history, more tightly patterned and compact, its thin air less swamped by pollution, its stockade of mountains steeper and chillier, its ancient centre both more European and more exotic. And above all, the people! Nearly everyone he interviewed piped up about what Sarajevo meant and why they must remain here. Self-effacing prophets of cultural tolerance, Sarajevans were convinced that the world would come to their aid because they, in their centuries'-old multiculturalism, represented the world's best hope. The Muslims he met ate pork and the Serbs and Croats were proud of their Jewish and Muslim in-laws. People boasted of their Hungarian or Roma grandparents, or described their ancestry as too tangled for them to define themselves other than as Bosnians. Everyone seemed to be a doctor, a lawyer, a teacher, a professor, a classical musician or a poet. He spoke to them as, scavenging for surplus water that smelled of gasoline, they lined up with their transparent plastic bottles next to the tanker truck that pulled in at the back of the Holiday Inn. As they realized that the world was not going to help them, they grew more intense in their need to publicize their dilemma. People appeared at Darryl's hotel room unbidden, demanding to be interviewed: a Serbian army captain who had chosen to fight with the Bosnians, firing back at his own relatives to defend the multicultural society he believed in; a man who wished to tell Darryl that it was only after three weeks of sheltering in the cellar at night that the residents of his small apartment block had noticed that every couple in the building represented some sort of mixed marriage; a Sephardic Jew who had scheduled his "return" to Spain for the 500th anniversary of his ancestors' expulsion from the country in 1492.

By late 1993, once it had become clear that the world understood what was being done to Sarajevo and did not plan to stop it, the mood changed. The city's Jewish population, its hillside graveyard desecrated by the trenches dug by Serb artillery units, emigrated en masse. The people Darryl interviewed, the Sarajevans he had got to know, lapsed into a bittersweet Mitteleuropa irony. Of course we will be defeated, they said. Of course we will die. That is our role. We are the living form of all that the world's will to power must subdue. We are the antithesis of globalized sameness. But we are still here. They said we could not survive more than a few weeks . . . They bolstered their glorious defeatism with allusions to the Austro-Hungarian Empire, classical music, philosophers and writers whose names were no more than remote echoes in Darryl's ears. He felt a yearning to step aside from journalism and learn more about culture. He tried to think of artists he had met. In truth he had known few such people. His two nights talking to Paul in Havana circled back in his memory. He remembered how Paul had seemed not so much unaware of history and politics as insulated from these stresses by his ability to imagine sound.

During those early years male and female journalists had slipped into each other's rooms for the night at a more frantic pace than usual, wrapping their bodies together as bomb blasts shook the foundations of their hotels. Darryl could not recall when he had first noticed Hilde, from Belgian television. One night they found their way up to his room over the lobby of the Holiday Inn, and from then on they shared his bed. The intimacy of fear was accentuated by the intimacy enforced by malfunctioning toilets, sputtering showers and blackout darkness. Romance fell away: within days of stripping each other naked, they were relying on one another with the hard-nosed frankness of an old peasant couple. After lovemaking, if the water was running, they would stand side by side in the bathroom in sock feet, their bodies draped in rough blankets, as they washed out their condom for reuse tomorrow. When they wore out the last condom their lovemaking became more tender in its limitations. After Hilde discovered there were no more tampons in Sarajevo, they scoured the city together in search of the inadequate wads of cotton used by many local women. Food shortages grew more severe; yet the Holiday Inn's frigid dining room — formerly its conference centre — continued to serve three institutional meals a day. In search of variety, Darryl and Hilde joined the suicidal dashes in armoured cars through the front lines to the black-market town of Kiseljak, where steak and fruit, like champagne, gasoline and ammunition, were on offer to all who carried Deutschmarks or dollars. They feasted on the spoils in bed, their breath rising before their faces as they chewed. They spoke in French, the second language they shared, making plans to settle down in Montreal or Paris and write uncompromising books about Bosnia. In the cold, strange air of a night sky inked out by mountains their schemes acquired the force of inevitability. After they had been together for a year and a half — nearly an endurance record in Darryl's incessantly interrupted emotional history — Hilde was posted to South Africa to cover Nelson Mandela's accession to power. The culture they had created in the high-flung den of his room evaporated. Hilde's voice over the line from Johannesburg, on the rare occasions when he got through to her on the satellite phone, had a choppy Dutch accent. They spoke in English, she greeting his talk of Muslims, Serbs and Croats with increasingly committed accounts of Afrikaners and Zulus. Long before she lost interest in his calls, he felt betrayed. She had forgotten that nowhere on earth was as important as *here*.

Rick, too, lived for Sarajevo's importance. Darryl had avoided him at first. Ten years younger than he, brasher and more cynical and, Darryl sensed, better educated and better paid — American, in short, in a way Darryl found irritating — Rick had reported on every crisis on earth and had been affected by none. He was a cynic converted by Sarajevo into an enraged idealist. Nothing before had touched him. He had a wife in Chicago whom he casually betrayed, two children he barely acknowledged, parents in Minnesota he had not seen in three years. He had dropped his first two employers overnight for better offers.

"Hey, Canuck!" Rick called from the bar one day in the early summer of 1992. "Darryl Sittler! How come you guys don't send a hockey team over here? The way they fight, they'd finish off Karadžić and Milošević in ten minutes."

Against his better judgement, Darryl sat down. It was the beginning of their friendship. In his whining upper-Midwest voice that pronounced "when" as "win," burdened with the principle-laden diction that even the most worldly American never seemed to dispense with, Rick said: "What the *fuck* is going on here? I mean, does this place make sense to you? The Europeans recognize Slovenia and Croatia, so that means they have to recognize Bosnia. Bosnia has an elected multi-ethnic congress and a clean independence referendum, and the Serbs just walk out of it and pick up their guns. And most of the Serbs on the ground don't even want to pick up guns — it's Milošević back in Belgrade pushing for more territory and that nutcase shrink Karadžić with his half-baked racial stuff. But they get the whole fucking Yugoslav army behind them and take over two-thirds of the country and what does the goddamn U.N. do? It slaps an arms embargo on the Bosnian government so they can't fight back! And then my editor in Chicago tells me I've got to change my articles to say what's really happening here is 'warring factions' and 'all sides are equally to blame.' Fuck equality! I never thought I'd hear myself say that, you know? But there is no equality. This isn't 'warring factions,' it's an invasion! A few dozen cops and crooks and weekend soccer players shooting back with pistols and hunting rifles and old Kalashnikovs and a couple of howitzers against the fifth-biggest army in Europe. And that's only happening here in Sarajevo; everywhere else you go, except maybe Srebrenica and Bihać, there's no resistance — just Muslims putting their heads down and getting it in the neck. Objectivity's great, but sometimes objectivity means telling people who's doing the goddamn killing."

"Your State Department says ethnic cleansing isn't happening."

"Yeah, Milošević met all the big-money boys when he worked in New York for Beobanka. He's been real careful to send Yugo America car contracts to Deputy Secretary of State Eagleburger and National Security Adviser Scowcroft and former Secretary of State Kissinger. Of course they're soft on Milošević! He's part of the military-industrial complex!"

"It's been a long time since I heard anybody talk about the military-industrial complex."

"I didn't invent it," Rick said. "Eisenhower invented it. And he was a Republican."

The next week they travelled up to Croatia to interview refugees coming over the border from northern Bosnia. For most of the last five hundred years, much of the population of northern Bosnia had been Muslim. Now the only remaining Muslims were in concentration camps. Darryl and Rick got permission from the Bosnian Serb Army to cross the border into Bosnia to visit the town some of the refugees had come from — a beautiful town, they were told, full of historic buildings. When they got there, they could not find the town. At last they realized that the fields they were walking through were sown with shards of stucco and stone; the grass was cut with broad tread marks and the occasional extra-wide path of mud. After a few minutes they came upon a row of surprisingly large houses with vacant windows and staved-in roofs. The rest of the town had been bulldozed: every building razed, nearly every scrap of rubble carted away.

"I don't believe this!" Rick shouted. "I don't fucking believe it. There used to be houses here, mosques, schools, a hospital, a library . . . Buildings that went back to the Renaissance, to the Middle Ages!" He ran in a circle, kicking at the shards of stone and stucco. He picked up stucco and hurled it onto the ground. A tinny clanking sound chimed up from the grass. "How can you just stand there?"

His voice wailed over the denuded plateau. Their interpreter was staring into space, while their two Serb military minders were lighting the cigarettes Rick had given them to dull their vigilance. They puffed out smoke from over long, imitation-Chetnik beards.

"I don't know what else to do," Darryl said. He was thinking that television could not convey the emptiness of a place where there was nothing to see. This was a tragedy no camera could report.

Denied permission to visit the death camp at Omarska, which the Serbs closed soon after the Bosnian camps hit the TV screens, they began to work through the official list of the ninety-four verified concentration camps (though new ones cropped up every day). Under close supervision, they were admitted to two camps. They tried to distract guards with cigarettes and plum brandy in order to take photographs, managing to abscond with a few clear long shots of gaunt men confined in cattle pens open to the sky. Some of the men were emaciated; these ones, they surmised, had been transferred from Omarska. At the end of the second day Darryl and Rick were told they were no longer welcome and escorted back across the border into Croatia. That was where the horror began.

Having been joined by an interpreter and a cameraman who had been sent down from Zagreb, they slept on cots in the back room of a school. The summer air was warmer and muggier than in Sarajevo, the nights smotheringly silent. All day they did interviews. The summer heat thickened the smell of the refugees' unwashed bodies. The first day's group had survived the camp at Brčko, where Serb irregulars had slit the throats of nine-tenths of the Muslims who had been herded into the camp three months earlier. They forced the survivors to drive the bodies to the grounds of an animal feed plant. Later in the day the feed plant's oven came on and the roiling stench sent the local population into their houses, where they hid behind closed windows and drawn curtains.

"This is insane," Rick said. He sat on his cot, the single bottle of Pilsener that he had paid through the nose for standing untouched at his feet. "This is the inferno. I don't want to know about this."

"Neither does anybody else. That's why we're here," Darryl said.

"When did you get so eager?"

"I just don't think we should leave yet."

The tension between them crested and fell as, day after day, they pushed each other back for one more session. Patterns emerged. Muslims had been imprisoned in tiny spaces where large numbers of people slept on their feet, drifting in and out of consciousness as their rations dropped to one daily piece of bread — sometimes, strangely, with jam — and one glass of water. They pissed and shit on each other's legs and feet until the smell itself became a kind of sickening nutrient that bore them in and out of their chafing, itching half-delirium. Beyond this similarity, every camp was different. In many, men's throats had been slit and their bodies rolled into the Sava River; in most, there had been prolonged beatings; in some, men were beaten to death and their bodies left to rot in the yard; in a few, Muslims who had been politically active were castrated with loops of wire in front of their families or neighbours.

Then there were the women.

Nearly every woman between the ages of fourteen and thirty had been raped. Older women had been raped if they were educated or married to wealthy men; but most of the victims were thin and very young. Devout Muslim girls from puritanical villages, those who were single had expected to remain virgins until elopement. Some had been raped by twelve men and some by one or two. Darryl and Rick met them after they had undergone pregnancy tests, and the gynecological examinations that confirmed their violation. They twisted on small, hard chairs, crying that they were ruined. They would never have children, no man would want them, the suspicion that they had gone with Serbs out of lust would always cling to them. Staring into their hard, stunned faces, observing their bare, unshaven legs and ill-spaced teeth, Darryl began to recognize repeated phrases. He wished he could break through the barrage of sound to understand what the women were saying before the interpreter's self-enforced deadpan sucked the feeling out of their words. He decided that when he returned to Sarajevo he would study the language that no one any longer wished to call Serbo-Croatian.

He heard his voice growing more strained as he whined out his questions. He was unable to sleep: the voices he could not understand kept chanting through his mind. He was tormented by indecipherable words relating unimaginable events. After eight days neither he nor Rick could continue. They found a driver to take them to Zagreb; from there Darryl broadcast to Canada. He didn't mind getting up three or more times a night to report to different Canadian time zones, in English and in French, because he was not sleeping anyway. He still wasn't sleeping a week later, when he and Rick hitched a ride back to Sarajevo on a Hercules participating in the U.N. airlift. In Sarajevo the crash of mortar shells restored him to a kind of deranged balance, drowning out the murmur of the voices. Months later he and Rick made double copies of their notes and photographs and, over a period of months, transferred these caches to their safety-deposit boxes in Toronto and Chicago. "We have a responsibility," Rick said, reinvigorated now that their ordeal was over.

Your responsibility. The days on the Croatian-Bosnian border could still haul Darryl awake at night, but it was Mohamed and Emina who dominated his memories. A few weeks before Darryl and Rick travelled to Croatia and northern Bosnia, the Yugoslav Army, in tandem with Karadžić's Bosnian Serb forces, had occupied Višegrad, where Mullah Hasanović had died in 1943. In the towns and villages along the Drina, Serbs and Muslims had remained neighbours, even friends, but in most other ways these places would have been unrecognizable to Mullah Hasanović. Tito had dammed the Drina to generate hydroelectric power; he had built paved roads, small factories and schools; television aerials prodded up from the villagers' houses. The arches built by Mehmet Pasha were complemented by new bridges that crossed the river gorge. When, nearly forty-nine years after Mullah Hasanović's death, Serb troops again invaded Višegrad, there were no Germans or pesky British advisers to distract them from the killing of Muslims. The towns along the Drina lay beyond the range of foreign television cameras: nothing that happened there would enter history. For more than two months, through June and July 1992, the Serbs killed every Muslim man they could seize. Mehmet Pasha's bridge became a crenellated embankment of death. Middle-aged men who had studied with Mullah Hasanović as boys, telling their sons about the rambling *hodža* who had taught them to read the Koran, were executed by the sons of Serbs with whom the Mullah had listened to *sevdalinkas* and shared legs of lamb. Children were pinned down flat on the asphalt by men who had watched them learn to swim the summer before, driven over with the treads of tanks and thrown into the river. A Muslim family found refuge in the shed of their Serb neighbours; when they were discovered, Serb paramilitary soldiers slit the Serb family's throats before killing the Muslims. They threw the bodies off Mehmet Pasha's bridge. The loudness of the splashing noise bodies made when they hit the water surprised everyone in Višegrad. So many throats were slit that the smooth white stones of the bridge hummed with flies. Women who had been locked up and raped were released from captivity to scrub away the blood and rotting body parts of their fathers, brothers and husbands. Still the bridge stank. Milan Lukić, the local Serb in charge of ethnic cleansing, ordered the floodgates of the hydroelectric dam opened to wash away the bodies. Hundreds of stiffened corpses rode the cascade of water around the deep bends of the Drina gorge. Human forms broke the surface of the black torrent to surge into the daylight for an instant before being engulfed again by the rush of water. Bodies careered off cliff-faces, battered remnants washed up hours later. Serb fishermen thirty kilometres downriver refused to drop their lines in the water for three years.

This was where Mohamed and Emina's story began. Darryl had reported on the ethinc cleansing in eastern Bosnia at the time it occurred, nearly three years before he met Mohamed and Emina. He had reported on rumours of reports, had reported inadequately, standing in front of the Sarajevo Holiday Inn, without understanding the magnitude of what was happening or the fact that it was happening in part because it had happened before. After he and Rick had taken off for Croatia to report on northern Bosnia, he had shuttled events in eastern Bosnia to the back of his mind until the refugees began to swarm into Srebrenica.

Twelve thousand Muslims had been living in Višegrad. Two thousand had been murdered and ten thousand fled. Some got away as soon as they realized what was about to occur; others, successfully concealed by Serb friends, had slipped through the Army's lines at night. In all the towns and villages along the Drina, the experience was similar. By August there were no more Muslims. The refugees were disproportionately female. Battles shunted them from place to place until, in late 1992, they began to pour into Srebrenica and the surrounding hamlets. In April 1993 the United Nations declared Srebrenica a "safe area" without defining its boundaries, and General Mladić's Bosnian Serb Army closed in to play cat-and-mouse with the thousands of refugees and the paltry contingents of peacekeeping forces — first Canadian, later Dutch — for the next two years. Local Muslims, regarding the refugees as a protective shield defending them against an otherwise inevitable invasion and slaughter, thwarted international efforts to get the refugees out. The stalemate required food drops to keep the encircled town alive.

Mohamed had seen it coming. At the beginning of 1992, weeks before Srebrenica was briefly captured by the Serbs, then retaken by a gang of enraged Muslim police officers, his father began to appear to him in dreams. He saw Mullah Hasanović on the road, striding through the hills in his leather boots and the fez that sometimes adorned his head. This time, though, as he struggled to focus on the tall gaunt figure that he had never seen in life, his father appeared to be walking away from the

Drina. Over his father's vanishing shoulders he could discern the mountain-ringed skyline of Sarajevo.

"We're getting out," he told Emina. "The Chetniks are coming and this time they aren't going to stop at the Drina."

"But our house! We can't abandon it."

"It'll be here for the people from the Drina when they arrive. And they will arrive . . . I know it's dangerous to travel to Sarajevo now, but soon it will become impossible. We're luckier than most. We can live in my brother's house. He's moving his business to Ljubljana. He'll never go back to Sarajevo."

She looked at him with an expression in which fear and distrust mingled. "Why do you want to live in Sarajevo? Are you bored in the village? Are you bored with your wife and family?"

"Emina!" he said. "I want to save our lives! Please trust me!"

She looked at her feet and said nothing.

Darryl experienced the buildings reaching above him as a source of frustration. As he crossed the Goetheplatz, the number 6 tram to Buchenwald clanked up against the curb. Why had he refused Magdalena? It would lead to nothing, as adherence to principle invariably led to nothing, and in the meantime he had ruined a friendship and lost the opportunity to spend the night with a beautiful woman. At his age he could not expect to receive many more offers. As he passed the oversized statues of Goethe and Schiller presiding over the deserted Theaterplatz, and turned down Schillerstrasse in the direction of Park an der Ilm, it struck him that perhaps he no longer cared.

He unlocked the door and pressed the timed light at the bottom of the stairs. The light went out as he approached the apartment. He stepped inside and listened. Nothing. He padded down the hall in the track shoes he had worn to the concert, conscious of the creeping stiffness in his forearms, calves and shoulder blades. He passed his door, reached Nikolai's door and stopped. At the top of the door was a glass-panelled transom: the lights in Nikolai's room were off. He visited the kitchen, the bathroom, and followed the crooked corridor past the trays of scrap metal to the toilet at the back of the building. No one. Hardly believing that only a few hours ago the apartment had been thronged with people and multilingual argument, he returned to his room and went to bed.

The chords of Paul's music raced through his mind as he fell asleep. The sounds unlocked memories of refugees' indecipherable voices. When the door of his room opened, he sat up, uncertain whether this was a dream. Voices spoke to him in German; his mind remained trained on the English of Rick's fax. When he tried to speak his words emerged in Spanish. Two figures stooped over him; one of them turned on the lamp in the corner.

"No," the man's voice said. "You can't — "

"I have to talk to him," the woman said in the voice of a willful girl.

"But he's asleep. Please, Latifa. Let's go to my room. Tomorrow we can — "

"I want to talk to him now." She crossed the room from the lamp to the bed.

"It's okay," he said with a wave in Nikolai's direction. He swung his legs out of bed, realized he was wearing only underpants, and groped for jeans and a T-shirt. As they watched him dress he wondered whether young people found the sight of a middle-aged body intriguing in a repulsive kind of way. They themselves were sparingly clad. Latifa's blouse had come unbuttoned in front, exposing the tops of oblong white breasts, Nikolai's torso bulged against his T-shirt. Only after pulling his own shirt over his head did Darryl realize they were holding hands. Their bodies touched at the hip, the night heat gleaming on their bare, entwined arms.

"Did you really know my uncle?" Latifa said.

"I knew Mohamed and Emina Hasanović. Is that your father's brother and his wife?"

Nikolai's grip tightened as Latifa pressed her lips together. The Muslim and the Jew, was the first thought to pass through Darryl's mind. In their broad-shouldered, dark-eyebrowed height, they both appeared Slavic. And young. Nikolai must be six or seven years older than Latifa, but at the moment the difference barely showed.

"Can you tell me about them?"

"Latifa," Nikolai said, tugging on her arm.

She reached over and kissed him. "My father won't let us talk about this."

She shook her hand loose, stepping free of Nikolai's grasp, then tucked her arm around his waist. Darryl saw two tantalizing activities — sex with Nikolai and talking about the subject her father had banned — competing for her attention. Nikolai's pained expression made clear that, however swiftly Yury had been forgotten, he and Latifa had not yet gone to bed together.

"What do you mean your father won't let you talk about this?" Darryl asked.

"Latifa!"

"First I will hear what this man has to say, then we will go to your room."

"You think you can have everything," Nikolai said. "Sometimes you have to choose."

"Don't be mean to me," she said, seating herself on a wicker chair next to the Robotron computer propping up the pot in which the jade plant grew. The chair creaked beneath Latifa's weight. Her legs stretching across the hardwood in front of her, she kicked off her high-heeled clogs. "When we arrived in Ljubljana my father said: 'We're Slovenian now. We're never going to be Bosnian again. Ljubljana is our home. I don't want to hear a word spoken about the past in this house.' He even thought about making us take Slovenian names. I think he would have done it if his trucking business weren't so well known."

They began to learn Slovenian, a language mercifully distinct from the borderless mush of Serbo-Croatian-Bosnian-Macedonian-Montenegrin, yet an easy language to learn for a family accustomed to the unnameable tongue. Within a year they were speaking Slovenian at home. "The only hard part is when I sign my name. Especially if I get back from the disco at five o'clock in the morning! Sometimes I forget and sign in Cyrillic. When I sign in Slovenian — in the Latin alphabet — it doesn't look like my name."

Nikolai, kneeling at her side, reached up and stroked Latifa's arm.

"But what about your family in Bosnia? Don't your parents want to know about them?"

"They try to find out what's happened, but they don't tell my sister and me. They just want us to have a good time. Even when I go out to the disco and come home at ten o'clock in the morning and it's obvious I've been with some boy my father smiles. I know he's thinking about how if we had stayed in Bosnia I might be dead, and I know he'll let me do almost anything." Her smile grew huge. How excessively pleased she was with her ordinary good looks, Darryl thought, and how unaware of their ordinariness. Her wide mouth pursed. "About once a year a relative comes to visit and we all speak . . . the other language . . . for a day. The next morning we look at each other as if we've committed some sin. It's difficult to start speaking Slovenian again. I feel bad all day. It's like a hangover, only in my heart."

"You can't be ruled by the past," Nikolai said, resting his hand on her shoulder. "If I spent all my time worrying about who is Russian and who is Ukrainian and who is Jewish, I would go mad. We must put the past behind us!"

Fearing that Nikolai was on the brink of sidetracking the conversation, Darryl sought out his eyes. Nikolai looked contrite. In some fashion that they both sensed yet which Darryl could not put his finger on, Nikolai's pursuit of Latifa had contravened their unspoken pact as apartment mates.

The room grew as still as the empty park across the street.

"Sometimes," Latifa said, "I feel as if I'm having fun because my parents want me to have fun. Like I'm doing it for them. Then I get mad at them for trying to hide things from me. But even when I get mad I don't say anything because I'm afraid of hurting my father. I just have another drink."

"So you don't know about Mohamed and Emina?"

"I don't know anything! Their oldest son — he's my oldest cousin — came from Germany last year, but he only stayed for lunch and my parents didn't let him talk to to my sister and me about anything except his job in Frankfurt."

"I knew Mohamed and Emina in Sarajevo. If you want — "

"No!" Nikolai said, getting to his feet. "No more! I grew up hearing about the wonderful Soviet Union, now I must hear about the horrible war in Bosnia. Why can't we forget these things?"

He left the room. Latifa jumped to her feet.

"Where are you going?" Darryl asked.

The rim of flesh between the bottom of her tight blouse and the top of her flared slacks pouted as she stopped in the doorway. "I'm going to bring him back. He needs to hear this, too."

Late in the siege, Sarajevo changed. The professors and poets and sophisticated lawyers and humane doctors and worldly classical musicians trickled away to Austria, Germany, Sweden, Canada. The educated, peace-loving idealists gave up on saving their multicultural paradise and in their place Muslims ethnically cleansed from eastern Bosnia flooded in: Muslims who scorned mixed marriages, observed the call to prayer from any surviving mosque and would not touch bacon; ex-Yugoslavs, ex-Bosnians, ex-Europeans, who had learned from oppression that their defining trait was their religion. Darryl sensed the change when he glimpsed the first veiled women in the market. Aching for female company as the months since Hilde's departure passed, he calibrated the difference between the old and new Sarajevans by observing their daughters. The daughters of the old Sarajevo Muslims went to university, spoke foreign languages and slept with their boyfriends, who were as likely to be Serbs, Croats, Hungarians or Jews as other Muslims. The daughters of the country people, whom the old Sarajevans denigrated as "Swedes," spoke archaic highland dialects, were pulled out of school at thirteen and locked in back rooms until, at seventeen, they managed to elope. The Swedes brought their devotion and despair with them to Sarajevo, embracing anyone who offered support. Posters of Iranian spiritual leaders sprouted on the walls of the old city. The Bosnians from the countryside fought better than the city sophisticates. The Bosnian Army, created then enlarged in defiance of the U.N. arms embargo, was beginning to win battles in northern and central Bosnia. Later that year, Serb gangs would rampage through Serbian neighbourhoods. Thousands of people who had remained in Sarajevo because they considered themselves Bosnians first and Serbs second were herded into the countryside to populate the ethnically cleansed ghost towns of the psychiatrist Karadžić's racially pure Bosnian Serb Republic.

In his room pitched high above the foyer of the Holiday Inn, Darryl felt as trapped as the Muslim girls in their hillside *mahalas*. Having gone freelance to avoid being posted elsewhere, he could barely pay the Holiday Inn's siege-rate fee of US $60 a day for room and board. The world was growing tired of the destruction of Bosnia. Patches of rust blemished the white armoured cars of the U.N. Protection Force, UNPROFOR. Most of the daredevil foreign correspondents of 1992 and 1993 — Roy from *Newsday*, Ed from *The Guardian*, Peter from the *Washington Post*, Samantha from the *Boston Globe*, even Rick from Chicago — had left. Those who remained, like Darryl, had bags under their eyes and receding hairlines. They travelled outside the city less than they had in the past, and rarely ventured beyond the hideous yellow walls of the Holiday Inn unless saddled up in their flak jackets. The body count on Sniper's Alley, in front of the hotel, had never been higher. People no longer ducked or ran, or took detours to avoid the street. Sarajevans seemed not to care any more, seeking death as a way of ending this nightmare. Bosnian government snipers, in an attempt to attract the world's sympathy, joined the Serbs in shooting down Bosnian pedestrians. Sick with desperation, Darryl refused to retreat. He could not find an honourable way out.

The message from Mohamed and Emina was left at the front desk: *Come and see us tomorrow,* it said in German, *we're leaving the next day.* Darryl's depression deepened. Then his journalist's instincts clicked in. There might be a story here: Mohamed and Emina were not originally from Sarajevo. They were country people, in spite of their prosperity and Mohamed's years in Austria. If even the country people were getting out of Sarajevo that would be something to write about.

Early the next morning, sweating in his flak jacket, he struggled up the muddy streets of the hillside *mahala* where Mohamed and Emina were living in the house of the older brother who had moved his family to Ljubljana. The view downhill as he glanced behind him was dominated by the rubble-clogged U of the river bending around the massive, shattered, gold-inlaid façade of the burned-out National Library, tomb of the incinerated history of Bosnian culture: tens of thousands of manuscripts in Serbo-Croatian, Turkish, Arabic and Persian

reduced to ashes by Serb incendiary rockets. He stared past
the low square houses climbing one upon another up the slope,
to the line near the tops of the mountains where the trees had
been razored away and the Serb mortars and Browning heavy
machineguns installed. Shattered stucco and toppled mailboxes
blocked the muddy street whose surviving cobblestones had
been flung like shrapnel against the walls of nearby houses.
The windowpanes had been replaced with the ubiquitous
UNPROFOR transparent plastic sheeting that appeared to be
the United Nations' only certifiable contribution to Bosnia's
well-being. A poster of Marshall Tito was captioned with a
mournful plea for the dead dictator to return. Darryl looked at
the poster and moved on, asking directions as he climbed.

Mohamed and Emina's older son, grown almost unrecog-
nizably gangly and sombre, greeted him at the gate. They
passed through the small, walled-in garden and entered the
open front rooms of the house. In observance of local etiquette,
Darryl removed his shoes at the door. Mohamed was wearing a
suit. Darryl still could not accustom himself to the unbearably
funereal aura of men's dress in the Balkans: the dark shirt and
tie beneath a dark jacket. Mohamed smiled at him. "My friend,
I am so glad you have come," he said in German. "We wish to
see all our friends before we leave Sarajevo. You will stay to eat,
of course."

Before Darryl could demur, apprehensive that he might be
cutting into a scarce stock of food — a few weeks earlier the city
had been threatened with starvation — Emina appeared from
the closed-off back rooms, which visitors did not enter. A sprig
of grey glinted in the dark waves of her hair. Darryl noticed
that she was wearing baggy *dimije*; the two times they had met

socially since the interview in his hotel room, Emina had been wearing a skirt. She responded to his scrutiny with a lowering of her frank dark gaze. Their hands, clasped in an informal shake, clung to one another a second too long. Mohamed stepped forward. "We leave tomorrow."

"You're going back to Austria?"

"No, to Srebrenica."

"Pardon?" Darryl felt himself move back a step. He was too stunned to take off his flak jacket. "You're joking, of course." His attempt at laughter met with silence. "You can't. It's surrounded."

Mohamed's tall figure made him conscious of Emina's bowed head and folded hands. The boys were lounging on the couch in front of the stereo left behind by Mohamed's brother's family. "It's a U.N. safe area. Soon the war will end and it will become a Muslim enclave. The Chetniks can't have all of eastern Bosnia to themselves, it's never been that way before. I want to be there when the rebuilding starts. Our village is inside the safe area, so there's no danger. Obviously there will be refugees living in our house. But we will share it with them until the war ends."

Darryl turned around, stepping out of his flak jacket. One of the boys carried it to the door and set it down next to the family's shoes and boots. "But you can't get to Srebrenica — "

"There's a route open. People go in from Žepa with pack-horses through the hills over Zlovrh. They take in cigarettes, gasoline, toothpaste . . . Both sides know about the route and allow it to stay open."

"But how are you getting to Žepa? There are Serb roadblocks. You'll be killed!" Darryl noticed the cartons of Marlboro stacked in the corner of the room. Cigarettes: the currency of Srebrenica. In the refugees' half-starved anguish, even the swaggering Deutschmark had lost its clout.

"We have a ride to Žepa," Mohamed said. "Guaranteed."

"How much did you pay for that?" When Mohamed failed to reply, Darryl said: "They'll take your money and kill you." He glanced towards Emina. She avoided him, returning to the back rooms. Switching to Serbo-Croatian, Darryl said: "What do your children think about this?"

"They make fun of us here," the older boy said. He was beginning to grow a moustache. "They laugh at the way we talk."

"I thought you could get great CDs in Sarajevo," the younger boy said. He wore his hair spiked. "But it's lousy here. They say you can buy CDs in Kiseljak and in the Serb neighbourhoods, but you can't go to those places, so what's the use? When we came here there wasn't even any electricity."

"But now there is electricity."

"Yeah," the boy said, "and there's this great rock song about Srebrenica they play on the radio. If I went there I'd be the coolest guy in my class."

"I go to Kiseljak sometimes," Darryl said, struggling to form his sentences. The truth was that he had not visited the black-market town since Hilde's departure. "I'll bring you CDs the next time I go."

The boy looked away. Darryl stepped towards him. "Do you like CDs in English? American music?"

The boy met his eyes. "I like our music better."

Emina, emerging from the back rooms carrying a pot of soup, dealt Darryl a furious frown. They sat down and ate: soup and salad, followed by a breaded veal cutlet and *lonica*, a peppery stew served in a clay pot with a tight-fitting lid. Darryl had heard of *lonica*, but this was the first time he had eaten it. They drank the thick Turkish coffee, replete with *caimac*, that he had last sipped in the company of a Serbian officer who had lectured him on the "foul Turkish culture" of Bosnian Muslims. After a long silence, he prodded Mohamed again. "You won't be eating *lonica* in Srebrenica."

"We do not usually eat *lonica* in Sarajevo. It's taken us weeks to find the food for this meal."

Darryl felt guilty, though he knew Mohamed's concept of hospitality precluded this intent. "In Srebrenica you'll be running up hillsides into sniper fire, fighting with hundreds of other people over the contents of a wooden box dropped by parachute. That's how you'll get your food. There's no soap, there's no shampoo, there's no medicine if you get ill or if you're wounded."

"We will be at home in our house," Emina said.

"Darryl." Mohamed laid his hand on the table. "I am beginning to think I misinterpreted the dream where I saw my father walking away from the Drina. I think now that this was not a signal but a reproach. My father's soul was abandoning me because he sensed my commitment wavering. He saw me trying to run away from my past. This war started because we ran away from our pasts. For fifty years we were not allowed to talk about what we did to each other during the Second World War. That was what gave Milošević and Tudjman their chance. If we'd been at peace with the past no one would have listened to those two madmen."

"Yes, but now it's too la — "

"It's not too late. It's time to go back. I will go on with the life my father left to me. That is my way of ending this insanity."

"Have you explained this to General Mladić?"

"Mladić will not attack. The war will end soon."

Darryl looked at his plate.

By the time they started dessert, an overgrown baklava and a rich flan, other visitors were arriving: country people from near Srebrenica, Muslims, Serbs and Croats from Sarajevo. Everyone realized the Hasanović family was leaving, though no one asked where they were going; most seemed to assume their destination was Germany or Austria. Darryl observed Emina's dark curls, Mohamed's broad, handsome, drooping, resolute face and the boys' straight backs as they greeted their guests and served them Turkish coffee. Their confidence unnerved him. Was this what a family was like? Not having been part of one in nearly twenty years, he wondered. Does one person's madness — the father's madness, usually — become a substitute reality? Can myths shared by four people become so strong that they rule out measured assessment of the world?

He took Mohamed by the arm and guided him into a corner, separating him from a well-wisher. The toe of his sock grazing a case of Marlborough cigarettes, he whispered in German: "You can't do this. It's too dangerous. Don't you realize that Mladić has been waiting his whole life for this chance?"

"Darryl, we will be surrounded by friends, protected by the United Nations — "

"He doesn't care about that," Darryl said.

A man in a black suit interrupted them before he could go on.

When he left Emina gripped his hand too tightly, a wave of feeling sheering up through her eyes. Mohamed and the boys shook hands with him. "You will come and see us when the war ends," Mohamed said.

Darryl returned to his round of watching the bodies pitching forward on Sniper's Alley from the window of his room in the Holiday Inn. He sold a documentary spot on the Islamicization of Sarajevo's women to a couple of networks and made enough money to pay his room and board for a few more weeks. The whistle of incoming mortar shells tore him from his sleep to half-recalled images of Mullah Hasanović plunging through space, his fez flying off his skull, parachuted food-drops crashing down towards Emina's outstretched hands, pinning her to the ground by her hair beneath the beech trees until every strand of her glossy locks turned grey, the dark circles beneath her eyes whirling into hubs of bare black earth where mosques had stood. In the mornings he dragged himself to the United Nations press briefings he had hated since his arrival. The purpose of U.N. briefings — indeed, the purpose of the U.N. mission in Bosnia — was to quell international calls for military action against the Serbs, which the United States, Britain, France and Russia, for different reasons, all wished to avoid. At each press conference U.N. officials stood up and explained that Serb forces were complying with cease-fire agreements by withdrawing from towns and cities that reports from the front lines insisted they were bombarding and overrunning. In earlier years U.N. officials had concocted a strange, twisted language, or feigned incomprehension of any language, to explain why the bulk of the international food aid intended for besieged Sarajevans was being delivered to Serb military commanders, or why U.N.

forces had handed over the Deputy Prime Minister of Bosnia, who they were meant to be protecting, to a Serb death squad for execution. Recently, a U.N. official had shuffled forward and declared that Sarajevo was not actually under siege. Darryl had watched three generations of Bosnia correspondents pass through the stages of solemn notetaking, scepticism, then outraged baying at the U.N. officials. Shortly after reaching the howling stage, most journalists left for another posting. Two years ago Darryl had been screaming at the despicable U.N. lackeys. His determination to remain in Sarajevo after Hilde's departure had turned his rage inward in the form of unresponsive, shellshocked surveillance. He observed without reacting. The pattern was unhealthy, but it was the only way he could stay here.

The day that Mladić's Multiple Launch Rocket System opened fire on Srebrenica, Darryl hunched over the short-wave radio with three other journalists. Mladić had appeared on Bosnian Serb television to announce that he had come to Srebenica for revenge. Now Serb mortars bombarded the observation posts of the Dutch U.N. peacekeepers protecting the town. Karremans, the Dutch commander, pleaded for NATO air strikes. NATO refused. For five days Mladić poured shells into Srebrenica at a rate of one mortar-round per minute. Karremans promised the terrified inhabitants that NATO air-strikes would destroy Mladić's forces. NATO flew two desultory sorties: the first blew up a Serb tank, the second got lost and failed to locate Mladić's army. Mladić threatened to kill Dutch peacekeepers he had taken hostage unless the air strikes were called off. Tanned, pudgy and relaxed from his summer of taunting NATO and the U.N., Mladić invited Karremans to have a drink with him.

The tall, grey-haired, worried-looking Dutchman toasted the fall of the U.N.'s safe area with the smiling Serb general while the television cameras rolled; the pictures went around the world. NATO backed down, and Mladić's T-54 tanks advanced. Darryl wore a path in the dingy carpet between his room and the press cockpit where the short-wave radio stood. In three days he wrote six articles and sold them all over the world. The elation he normally would have felt failed to stir. His choked panic throttled all other emotions. At the end of five days, Mladić halted the shelling. The next day, in suffocating July heat, the Serb forces overran Srebrenica. Darryl paced the halls of the hotel. Had Mohamed and Emina and the boys made it back to Mullah Hasanović's house, or had they all died weeks ago on their way home? He hoped they were already dead. It was obvious what was happening, even before U.N. spokes-people began downplaying the seriousness of the situation. Mladić had been building up to committing a massacre for decades. Darryl remembered Mladić's impatient silence at a press conference in Rogatica the year before, the second time he had seen the general in person. Earlier in the summer, as Mladić was laying his plans, his daughter had committed suicide at her university in Belgrade. Yet now he looked like a man on vacation. During the slaughter of the refugees streaming out of Srebrenica the general was everywhere, rushing from building to building, joking with the prisoners as they slumped towards execution, handing candies to children as their fathers were shot, overseeing the soldiers who locked up every Muslim man over the age of fourteen, then slit their throats, fired bullets into the backs of their heads, beat men to death with clubs out of the sheer pleasure of feeling a Muslim body crack bone by bone.

Thousands took refuge at the U.N. base at Potočari. When the Serbs entered the base, the Dutch peacekeepers handed over the Muslim men and boys to Mladić for execution. Prisoners were divided by regions, then Serbs from their home villages went in to say: "It's all right, I'll get you out. I'm your old neighbour, you can trust me." The men paraded onto the buses Milošević had sent from Belgrade to assist Mladić, and were never seen again. Nearby fields grew lumpy with their half-buried bodies. Those who fled in the direction of Konjević Polje, hoping to reach Muslim-held territory, were shot in the woods, or shot each other out of terror, or stepped on mines, or held grenades to their chests and pulled the pins when they saw the Serbs coming, or were rounded up by Serb military patrols and had their throats slit, or were rescued by blue-helmeted Dutch U.N. peacekeepers who turned out to be Serbs in uniforms they had taken from the hapless Dutch. Six thousand dead? 7000? 8000? While Washington sat on its hands, four US spy satellites scanned the wooded hillsides, counting the bodies.

The frenzy that had driven Darryl to work twenty-hour days during Mladić's opening bombardment yielded to dazed passivity. It was time to leave. Muslim civilization in eastern Bosnia — Mullah Hasanović's civilization — was finished. A month later, as the U.N. again turned a blind eye, the Croats drove a quarter of a million Serbs out of Croatia: refugees on tractors who putted away from the land where they had farmed since the 16th century. The officials in New York and Washington and Brussels and Moscow and Geneva looked at the maps and saw large swathes of territory with no minority populations. They knew that now they could enforce peace without risking a single dead foreign soldier.

Even the journalists who were losing their hair began to leave. Selling stories about Sarajevo became next to impossible, but Darryl kept trying because he had promised himself that he would not abandon Bosnia until he had found out what had happened to Mohamed and Emina Hasanović.

Only the next summer did he manage to fly to Tuzla and travel to Srebrenica. Two weeks later he returned to Toronto and tried to recover that remote experience that others referred to as a normal life.

He found a job as a feature writer on a Toronto newspaper, rented an apartment in the Annex and settled down to turn out pieces on what his editor, Barbara, described as "social trends." It all seemed to be a kind of forgetting: the forgetting of those who would never know there was anything to remember. Teenagers were piercing their bodies, marijuana was back in fashion among the middle classes, even schoolchildren were drinking cappuccino. "I love your irony," Barbara said, after editing his second piece. "You can tell that you realize all this stuff is a big zero."

Too late and with too much haste, he tried to pull together an ordinary life among a generation he had lost touch with since giving up his Quebec City posting for his first foreign assignment. He had a job, an apartment. To consecrate his inclusion in the world of Canadian ordinariness, all he needed was a mate, a "partner" as everyone now said. (To Darryl the word conjured up visions of Hollywood cowpunchers clapping each other on the shoulders.) It was time to put his nightmares behind him and form a relationship with a woman who would appreciate his good qualities. So acquaintances told him. Yet his relations with people in general, and women in particular, were abrasive and confused. The women he met classified him as immature because he had not settled down. Their parochialism angered him. The Ontario WASP censoriousness he had bristled against as a student persisted, recast as faux chic conformity. In the old days they had frowned at you for having long hair or not going to church; now they frowned at you for not wearing the right jacket, not expressing the right opinion about child-rearing, not drinking the right coffee; but the frowns were the same.

Bosnia kept coming back: it returned in the clench-jawed face of the media-friendly Canadian general who the people of Sarajevo had loathed more than any other peacekeeper; it dived back in jagged memories as Darryl read the evangelizing book Rick had written about US media coverage of Bosnia, recognizing himself in anecdotes and descriptions; abused, misconstrued, misrepresented, misunderstood, the word "Bosnia" intruded into every facile cocktail party or newspaper allusion to the distant world. He crept out of supernaturally smoke-free parties early rather than continue conversations that would have caused him to uncork screaming outrage or weeping despair. He paced the long arteries of Bloor and Danforth streets late at night, dazzled by the massed lights and the sleek, endlessly dining crowds who ate and ate without getting fat. People who would never understand, no matter how many times he told them about it, the feeling of watching a city being pulverized day by day for four years. He had to get this out of his system; he told Barbara he wanted to write about Bosnia. "That would be great," she said. "I'd like to think we could handle something a little more serious around here."

Acting on a telephone tip from a newspaper reader who remembered his television reports, Darryl visited a university to write an exposé on a professor who was running a course called "Representations of War," which was devoted to demonstrating that no Serb had committed any act of violence during the war in Bosnia. By sitting in on one of the professor's lectures, Darryl discovered that his primary source was an English translation of an article by a German journalist that had been published in a London magazine.

When he submitted his feature, Barbara cut it. "You can't say that," she said, pointing to a line on the screen. "And you can't say that, either."

"It doesn't matter that those things happened?"

"You say they happened."

"I say they happened because they're part of the historical record." He met Barbara's gaze and saw he was getting nowhere. "So what can I say?"

"You can say what other people say. You're a reporter. You report other people's words. Everybody has an opinion. You give your readers the different opinions and let them decide."

"So there's no truth? What if this professor was denying the Nazi Holocaust of European Jews?"

"That's different."

"Why is it different?" Darryl said. "Is it different because the victims are Jews and not Muslims? Or is it different because Auschwitz and Buchenwald happened at a time when we still believed in truth and Srebrenica and Omarska happened in a time when there are only different points of view? Does that mean that no genocide that occurs today can be remembered?

Does it mean we can no longer remember our history? Because if it does, we're all heading in the same direction as Yugoslavia."

Barbara was silent for a moment. "I know how you must feel," she said. Her voice sheered into a high-pitched laugh. "I mean, I've never lived through anything like that! But right now my worry is how you fill your quota for this week. Either you let me edit this piece into a form where we can run it, or you write me a feature on some other subject."

"Edit it," he said. "Just don't ruin it."

He left Barbara's cubicle. The article ran beneath the headline: *DEBATE OVER BOSNIA.* Darryl could barely read its infinitely qualified, on-the-one-hand-but-on-the-other-hand sentences. Having planned to fax a copy of the article to Rick, he ended up phoning him to explain why he didn't want to send it. "Hey," Rick said. "How's about I hop up to Toronto for the weekend? As long as I don't freeze my butt off."

"You're not going to freeze your butt off in May," Darryl said.

By the time Rick arrived, Darryl had begun to get reactions to his article. Toronto's Serb community, outraged by the NATO bombing of Belgrade in retaliation for a conflict in Kosovo that had killed only one per cent the number of people who had died in Bosnia, was revved up for protest. Darryl was assailed with hate mail and late-night anonymous phone calls that suggested that he was a lackey of Yankee imperialism, an agitator for Muslim holy war or a member of the international Zionist conspiracy. He stopped answering his phone. "I don't think I want to be a journalist any more," he said, when he picked up Rick at Pearson Airport.

Rick was bristling over the NATO bombing. "I can't believe it! If they'd done this over Bosnia in '92 they could have saved 200,000 lives. But no, they wait seven years and do it over goddamn miserable Kosovo." He stared at Lake Ontario heaving between the gaps in the unfinished stockade of condo towers lining the Gardiner Expressway. "You see they targeted the Yugo car plant? That was a pretty clear message to banker Milošević. No more buying off boys in the State Department by sending them Yugo contracts. Milošević just got expelled from the military-industrial complex. That's what this bombing is about."

They wrangled for the rest of the weekend. The crest of blond hair that used to fall into Rick's eyes when he needed a trim had shrivelled to a frizzy, carefully barbered spear extending to the brink of the top-shelf line crossing his forehead. His features had thickened and his voice had grown creakier. After leaving Bosnia he had taken a year off to write his book, been divorced by his wife, quit journalism, worked for an international aid organization, then slithered back into newspaper work through the local beat on a Chicago daily. From there it had been a short step back into being a foreign correspondent. He had started out by covering the efforts to bring to trial for libel the British historian who denied the Holocaust and the London magazine that had printed the German article denying Serb ethnic cleansing. From there he had moved on to Germany. He had just returned from writing a series on eastern Germany ten years after the fall of the Berlin Wall.

"I wish I'd chosen some other line of work," Darryl said. "I'm sick of writing about cappuccino and dog-walkers, but

I don't think I could stand going back to reporting anything serious."

"Take a break," Rick said. "You need some time out. Quit your job, or take a year off if you can, and get away. In fact, if you want to do something totally mindless, in Germany I drank a Pilsener with this guy who's setting up the cultural program in Weimar this summer . . . "

～

"You haven't told me about Srebrenica."

Latifa twisted the rings on the fingers of her right hand. She and Nikolai sat cross-legged on the floor. Darryl stretched his legs in front of him, trying to loosen his stiff calves. In reality, there were many things he had not told Latifa. He had not divulged to her that her father had fought with the Ustasha as a teenager. This would have to come, but later: tomorrow, or the next day, or when the time felt right. It would be unfair to expose her to this sort of pain when what he had to tell her now would be hard enough.

The glimmer of her rings had softened. Looking over his shoulder he saw, through the leaves of the jade plant, the pre-light preceding the first seep of dawn. His aching legs gave him no relief. If he glanced in a mirror he would look grey-faced and old. "It was the next summer — the summer of 1996. I went to Tuzla first. There was an airport there and thousands of refugees in tents. The survivors, the people who had got away. Thousands of women, but lots of men, too. I found a list and Emina's name was on it."

"You liked her, didn't you, my Aunt Emina?" Latifa said. "I can tell by the way you talk about her."

"I felt something towards her," Darryl said. He saw Nikolai regarding him with a curious expression. Impatience had given way in his broad face to a kind of surprise. "I felt she had been betrayed — "

"I know how women are treated in my family," Latifa said.

" — betrayed in many different ways. By many different people." It was too painful to elaborate. He, too, had become one of Emina's betrayers. When he tracked her down she had sobbed on his shoulder. She was wearing a long T-shirt over a pair of baggy dungarees. The T-shirt was too large and the dungarees were too tight. He had never seen her hair so long. The strands she shook out of her eyes were grey. Her thinness showed up most in the hard veins rising from the backs of her hands. Having waited for this moment for a year, he was startled to realize they could scarcely communicate. Her rush of emotion exposed the inadequacy of his command of the unnameable language. He hired an interpreter and discovered that Mohamed, Emina and the two boys had been robbed on the journey from Sarajevo to Srebrenica. They had arrived in the safe area alive and unharmed, but as destitute as other refugees. They walked to their village and discovered fourteen people living in their house. The boys, who had welcomed the journey over Zlovrh with the pack horses as an adventure, said that they wanted to go back to Sarajevo.

Emina broke down. "My tall young sons," the voice of the interpreter, practised in siphoning out emotion, said. The faces of the other women in the tent were still.

When Mladić attacked, they had been rounded up and squeezed into a barn with perhaps two hundred other people. Serb soldiers came in and announced that men who were not

Arab terrorists would be given tickets on buses carrying them to safety. The women and children would remain in the barn until arrangements could be made to hand them over to the United Nations. The cut-off age for a child to remain with its mother was fourteen. Emina's older son was fifteen, the younger one thirteen. "But they were both very tall, with that accursed height they inherited from their grandfather. The Chetniks wouldn't believe that my younger boy was thirteen. They took them both. They called them Turks and Ustashas and *Balije*. Why couldn't they have left me one of my boys?" She grabbed Darryl's sleeve. "You must go look for them. They're still alive! They're hiding in the hills. They were athletic young boys. They could run fast. They ran away into the trees and the Chetniks never caught them."

The faces of the other women grew expressionless.

The second time he went to see her, he brought her bananas he had purchased from a black marketeer. She shared them with a grumpy older man in a long-billed cap. She told Darryl how she and the other women had been driven out of Srebenica in buses. Through the windows they had seen their men in the fields, sitting on their knees in formation with their hands clasped across the tops of their heads and armed Serb guards standing over them. Some of the guards forced the Muslim men to salute the buses carrying their wives and daughters with three-fingered Serb salutes. "I looked out the window the whole way," Emina said, "and I never saw my sons. That's how I know they got away." When the buses reached areas where there were no Muslim men in the fields, they stopped. One by one, every woman between the ages of fourteen and forty was taken out of the bus and raped by the side of the road. "I was crying so hard I looked old and ugly," Emina said.

She asked Darryl to help her get a visa to Canada. She did not want to spend another day in this country. "Here everything is a reminder of something else. I want to go to a country that has no history."

"A country where you have no history," he replied through the interpreter.

She ignored him. "Once I leave I will never come back." She watched the old man eat his banana. She edged away from him, hunching closer to Darryl, as though the interpreter made no difference. "If only Mohamed had let me move to Salzburg with him! Other Bosnian men took their wives to Salzburg. They got jobs serving food at the American boarding school there. They brought up their families in Austria. *Their* children are alive!"

Darryl felt ill. He wasn't sleeping. He worried about running out of time, and was chafing, in spite of himself, to visit the hillsides where the bodies of the victims had been rotting for more than a year. When he said he would work on her visa when he came back, it was obvious to them both that he was lying.

"We were betrayed by everybody, weren't we?" Latifa said. Nikolai laid his hand on her forearm; she shook it off. "No wonder my father doesn't want me to know about this. How can he tell me to pretend I'm Slovenian when all these horrible things have been done to us?" She drew an uneven breath and pulled her hair away from her face and shoulders. "Did you help her? Please tell me you helped her."

"I went away to visit the hillsides where the bodies were. There were three major sites. It was three days before I had time to visit Emina again. When I got there she was gone."

"Gone? Where did she go?"

"She ran away with the old man I saw in her tent. The other women said they were always together. The old man kept saying that if they got stuck in the camp, like refugees in other parts of the world, he would die of old age before anyone found them a home. Emina knew her husband and her boys were somewhere up in those hills, dead and unburied. In her lucid moments she knew it. She couldn't stand sleeping so close to where her family had been desecrated. She told one of the other women that if there had been a proper cemetery there, with headstones and identifiable bodies, she never would have left the area. But as it was, she couldn't stand staying there."

"How did she leave?"

"They started walking — she and the old man. The situation was too chaotic for anyone to go after them. Once they reached the highway they could have got a lift to Banja Luka and Bihać. From Bihać it was easy to get to Zagreb. Who knows how far they got? Maybe they're in Germany by now."

"But then my cousin, who came last year — " She stopped. "You'd think he'd know where his mother was."

"Did she know where he was?"

Latifa shook her head, her hair falling around her face. When Nikolai laid his hand on her bare arm she sagged into his embrace. "I don't know . . . " She looked up with a desolate expression that hauled him back to the camp at Tuzla. "I don't know anything, do I?"

"You can find out," Darryl said.

"And my Uncle Mohamed and the boys — there's no chance . . . ?"

"I really don't think that's possible."

"Did you find their bodies? I know that sounds sick, but I need to know."

"There was a moment where I thought I had found your uncle's body."

"Tell me about it."

"All right. But then you have to let me sleep."

In the pre-dawn light he saw Latifa glance at Nikolai. She reached up and turned off the lamp. She and Nikolai exchanged looks. Darryl could no longer tell whether they would stay together once they left his room: whether they would go to Nikolai's room and make love, whether Latifa would return to Göttingen or Ljubljana, whether they regarded each other with lust or affection or hatred. But the tired, wincing acceptance in their faces told him they knew they could not be indifferent to one another. Feeling that was enough, he told them about his walk in the hills.

Far into the distance, the rotting hillsides were flecked with white. The hide of the planet stank. Darryl sweated in the August heat. Mist hovered over the white-speckled dark green knolls. Double-treaded ruts showed where the Humvees had scaled the hillside when the Americans arrived, months later, to examine the scene. As they approached the edge of the forest of beech trees — another "beech wood," he thought, as he told them the story: another *Buchenwald* — the tall peasant Darryl had hired as a guide walked more and more slowly. When Darryl urged him on, he shook his head. In the back-country accent Darryl could scarcely make out, he said: "Not in there. It's a bad place. There are — "

"There are what?" Darryl said.

"Bad," the man said. "The devil."

"There are only the bodies of dead people. Dead Muslims."

The man grew angry. "Not dead Muslims! Only the Serbs suffer! Those are dead Serbs. Avengers of Kosovo! Warriors against the Ustasha Turks!"

Darryl paid the man his fee and walked into the woods. In the open areas, most of the bodies had been covered with a cursory layer of earth. Decay had stolen more quickly over the dead men in the forest. Twelve months had stripped them to clean, jaunty skeletons. There were skeletons clinging to tree trunks, skeletons crumbling into chalky piles, white spines beading the earth under the brambles. A bone snapped beneath his boot. His breath caught in his throat. He was looking at a tree where a man had been strung up in the branches. His wrists were wired to boughs high above his head. His arm- and shoulder-bones remained intact. Farther down the tree Darryl saw ankles and shafts of leg-bone trussed to the trunk with the same golden snare-wire. The skull, like the centre of the skeleton, had tumbled to the forest floor. The pieces lay around Darryl's feet. Closing his eyes, he saw the man's soul leaving his body as he hung dying above the cushion of dark green moss. He imagined the man's spirit falling through air as, months later, his bones would fall to earth.

Latifa stood up, tugging Nikolai to his feet. "Come on," she said. "Let's go. When we wake up, we'll visit Buchenwald. Then I'll think about what I do next."

Nikolai enclosed her in his long arm. His embrace had become less insistent. They walked out the door together, closing it behind them. When they had left, Darryl got up, undressed and lay down on his bed.

Two genocide trials in London next year. Buchenwald and Bosnia will both be on trial . . . Your participation . . .

Exhausted as he was, he couldn't sleep. He wished he could sit out under the trees in Park an der Ilm like lusty old Goethe and turn the moon in the clouds into a poem. He longed to have Paul's gift for transforming the air into sound. Or to be able to make dead matter yield energy, like Magdalena working with her silage. But he could do none of these things. He could only do his job. Some evening, he suspected, perhaps not that long in the future, Paul would turn on the television in a hotel room and see his old friend Darryl reporting from a war zone.

He drew a deep breath, overcome by drowsiness. He would answer Rick's fax when he woke.

NOTES AND ACKNOWLEDGEMENTS

In "The Killing Past," A.B. Chenvret's language is based on an interview with my great-grandfather, B.A. Glanvill, published in *The London Evening Standard*, April 13, 1936. I have also drawn on *Arthur and Mary Smith: A Family Tribute* (The Hallgate Press, 1991). I am in the debt of Eva-Maria Remberger for my initiation into the geography of Cologne. With regard to "A Grave in the Air," I thank Elizabeth Miles for making me return twice to former Yugoslavia and Emina Kadrić for offering hospitality in Sarajevo. I'm grateful to Diana Kuprel for checking my Polish. I thank Marlene Cookshaw, Elisabeth Harvor, Cristina Ionescu, Robin MacDonald and Andris Taskins for giving me useful suggestions on earlier drafts of some of these stories. I am extremely grateful to my editor, Seán Virgo, for making it possible for this book to benefit from his supernatural sensitivity to character and language. I thank Al Forrie and Jackie Forrie at Thistledown for continued support.

The personal story in "A Grave in the Air" is invented, but in addition to my own observations and conversations with Bosnians and other present and former Yugoslavs, I have drawn on many books, particularly *The Death of Yugoslavia* (Penguin, 1996) by Laura Silber and Allan Little, *Bosnia: A Short History* (Papermac, 1996) by Noel Malcolm, *The War in Bosnia-Herzegovina: Ethnic Conflict and International Intervention* (M.E. Sharpe, 1999) by Steven L. Burg and Paul S. Shoup, *Blood and Vengeance: One Family's Story of the War in Bosnia* (Penguin, 1999) by Chuck Sudetic, *Sarajevo, Exodus of a City* (Kodansha International, 1994) by Dzevad Karahasan, *A Witness to Genocide* (Macmillan, 1993) by Roy Gutman, *Love Thy Neighbor: A Story of War* (Knopf, 1996) by Peter Maass, *"A Problem from Hell": America in the Age of Genocide* (Basic Books, 2002) by Samantha Power, *Cuaderno de Sarajevo: Anotaciones de un viaje a la barbarie* (El País/Aguilar, 1993) by Juan Goytisolo, *Srebrenica: Histoire d'un crime international* (Médécins Sans Frontiers/L'Harmattan, 1996) by Laurence de Barros-Duchêne, *Srebrenica: Record of a War Crime* (Penguin, 1996) by Jan Willem Honig and Norbert Both, and three novels by Ivo Andrić: *The Bridge on the Drina, Bosnian Chronicle* and *The Woman from Sarajevo.*

Earlier versions of these stories, or sections of them, have appeared in *Prairie Fire, Carousel, Off the Shelf, The Antigonish Review* and *Queen Street Quarterly.*

STEPHEN HENIGHAN was nominated for a Governor General's Award in 2002, won a McNally Robinson Fiction Prize in 2004, and was a finalist for a National Magazine Award and a Western Magazine Award in 2006. He is the author of three novels and two previous short story collections. His stories have been published in Canada, the US, Great Britain and Europe. He is a columnist for *Geist*, and a contributor to magazines such as *The Walrus, The Times Literary Supplement, Matrix* and *Canadian Notes & Queries*. Henighan teaches Spanish American literature in the School of Languages and Literatures, University of Guelph.